Easter in Edinburgh

The Holiday Adventure Club Book Three

Stephanie Taylor

Chapter 1

April 10

Amelia Island, FL

It was almost time to leave again, and Lucy had barely gotten her feet in the sand and her body back on Florida time.

"You ready to hit the road, gorgeous lady?" Honey Joplin asked with her back to Lucy as she opened a new box of nail polish.

"I'm as ready as I'll ever be," Lucy admitted. She was seated at one of the manicure tables, waiting to see what new product Honey had ordered to replace the things she'd lost when her nail salon was broken into just a few weeks prior.

"How about purple with glitter?" Honey pulled a bottle of polish out of the box and set it on the table for Lucy to examine.

"Um...I think I'm more of a hot pink kind of girl," Lucy said, handing it back. "Do you have anything that looks like a highlighter? I was thinking of super short nails with really bright color."

Honey turned her back on Lucy again and opened up a different box. "Got it," she said, brandishing a brightly colored bottle. Honey had a slight hobble to her walk, but at nearly seventy, she was as spry as they came. "Let's get these nails looking vacation-ready, and while I'm doing that, you can tell me all about you and that cutie patootie next door."

1

"Honey!" Lucy set her hands flat on the manicure table as Honey switched on the lamp she used to examine her customers' cuticles. "There's nothing to tell."

Honey picked up one of Lucy's hands and dropped it again. She gave her a long, hard look. "Listen, girly. You can't kid a kidder, and you can't fool old Honey. I see you and Nick together and I know without a shadow of a doubt that there's something going on there. Now, do you want me to ask graphic questions, or do you want to spill the beans while I make you beautiful?" She opened a drawer and pulled out a nail file and a box that held a pair of sterilized cuticle scissors.

"Okay, okay," Lucy relented, picking up the bottle of nail polish she'd chosen and turning it over in her hand. It was called *Pink Panties for the Princess*. This made Lucy smile. "Things are good between us. We've been seeing each other since the trip to St. Barts, and I think I really like him."

"You think so?" Honey asked mildly, slipping on a pair of reading glasses and picking up Lucy's left hand so that she could trim and file her nails. "A man who writes wonderful books, patiently helps old people mail boxes home to Ohio, and runs around the island with a sweet dog, and you *think* you really like him?"

Lucy looked out the window at the palm trees that lined the parking lot of their little strip mall. Her battered and well-loved yellow VW Bug sat next to a giant monster of a truck, and the sun glinted off the back window, making her blink until she had to look away.

"There's so much more to him," Lucy finally said, letting Honey guide her hands into two bowls of warm, lavender-scented water. "We really got to know each other on St. Barts, and when we were together it was just easy, you know?"

Honey looked at Lucy over the top of her glasses. "Hey, there's nothing wrong with a man who is easy to be around. I've been with my share of easy ones, and I've been with just as many difficult ones.

Sometimes the difficult ones are better in the sack, but they're the ones who give you all the gray hairs. It's a trade-off."

Lucy laughed. "Fair enough."

She glanced around Honey's salon, which had been pretty much set back to the way it was after the wreckage the burglar had left in his trail. The front window had been replaced, the shelves that had held all of her polish were re-hung on the walls, and half of the boxes of product were on display there, the colors spread out like a rainbow. A few of Honey's hanging plants had been torn down and tossed unceremoniously to the ground, but she'd re-potted them and put the place back together admirably. Frankly, she appeared unshaken by the whole thing. The first thing she'd said to Lucy up on her return from St. Barts was, "Never let 'em get the best of you, kid. Always come back swinging."

"But my real question," Honey said now, drying off one of Lucy's hands so that she could apply the first coat of polish, "is how the other one is handling all of this canoodling? Are you two being discreet?"

"The other one?" Lucy's forehead wrinkled slightly.

"Oh, don't give me that," Honey said, shaking her head. "You know that Mr. Lopez is *not* a fan of what's happening between you and Nick."

Dev, Lucy thought. *Of course.*

"Well, he hasn't mentioned it, but it's not like he and I had anything going, Honey. He took me to an outdoor concert after I got back from Venice, but he never even tried to kiss me. And Nick and I have more in common than Dev and I do."

"That so?" Honey asked, hunched over Lucy's nails and spreading the shocking pink onto her middle finger with careful strokes.

"Sure," Lucy said, looking out the window again as a FedEx truck pulled up and parked in front of The Carrier Pigeon for its daily delivery and pick-up at Nick's postal store. She tried to think of the words to describe how she and Nick were just better suited to one another than she and Dev, but she couldn't come up with anything. "I guess it's more that Dev is just hard to access. Or something." She frowned.

"No, I hear you." Honey dipped the brush in the bottle and started on Lucy's other hand. "A man that quiet and mysterious is like Fort Knox."

"How so?"

"You can't penetrate him. He doesn't crack. There ain't no easy way in. But," she said, capping the bottle of polish and giving it a good shake before she started the next layer, "he *does* seem bothered by you and Nick."

"Oh, he does not," Lucy scoffed. "He sells me my coffee and talks business with me just like before."

"Well I flat-out asked him what he thought of you and Nick, and I could tell he didn't like it one bit."

"Honey!" Lucy nearly shouted. "You did not!"

Honey shrugged and lifted Lucy's left hand for the next coat of polish. "Sure I did. I'm old, I can get away with just saying what's on my mind."

Lucy dropped her chin and closed her eyes, praying for patience.

"This actually makes me glad that I'm about to leave town again," Lucy said, inspecting her freshly painted nails.

"Sure thing, girlfriend. You leave town, and let these two boys fight it out over you while you're gone." Honey opened a drawer and pulled out a bottle of clear topcoat.

"That is *not* what I need, Honey."

"Two hot men tussling with each other to see who wins your affection? Lucy Landish, every woman needs that—it's a boost to the morale. A reminder that you're alive and desirable." Honey finished up the topcoat and capped the bottle with a flourish. "Let them be men, and you just go on about your business being the stunning woman that you are."

Lucy couldn't help but laugh. "Okay, Honey. I think I can manage that." She left her fingers splayed on the table top so as not to smudge them. "Any last minute psychic messages for me before I hit the road again?"

Honey frowned for a minute, narrowing her eyes as if communing with the spirits, which it was quite possible she was actually doing, given the fact that her "messages" had come true in one form or another on more occasions than Lucy could count. "I did have a dream about Scotland the other night," she said. "There was a man who kept thinking he could save everyone—does that mean anything to you?"

Lucy shrugged. "Not yet. Other than the part about Scotland, anyway. But I'll keep my eyes peeled for some guy trying to be a hero."

"A hero. I think that's what they all want to be." Honey smiled. "And yet so few of them are," she added wistfully.

Lucy stood up and gave Honey a quick hug with her hands outstretched to protect the fresh polish.

"I'll see you when I get back." She blew Honey a kiss.

"Happy trails, señorita," Honey said, blowing her a kiss in return.

Chapter 2

April 12

Edinburgh, Scotland

Lucy was up to her eyeballs in bagpipes and plaid. She'd been in Scotland for less than twenty-four hours, and already she was getting used to the thick accent that had at first tripped her up during even the briefest interactions.

"Get you a wee bit more, lass?" a woman in a plaid skirt asked, bending forward at the waist as she leaned over Lucy's table.

"Please," Lucy said, pushing her teacup and saucer toward the hostess, who topped her off with a steaming brew poured from an antique-looking white ceramic pot painted with delicate flowers. "And thank you."

Lucy was seated at a small, round wooden table next to a window in the lobby of her hotel, looking out onto the rainy street from behind a pair of plaid curtains held back with iron hooks. Outside in the gray afternoon, the headlights of small, boxy cars cut through the gloom, and people walked about, heads bowed against the rain, ducking in and out of the shops and stepping on and off the red buses.

Lucy held a pen in one hand as she sat there with her tea and a notebook, jotting down last minute notes before the new group of travelers arrived. This trip was a stark contrast to her last one, and she marveled for a moment at the wildly different places she'd chosen to visit so far. While the gorgeous hotel she'd stayed at in St. Barts had been fully modern and with sumptuous views of the water and the sky, this hotel was all warm wood, fireplaces, and overstuffed plaid chairs and couches. There were paintings on the wall of horses racing across meadows, and in the hallway just off the lobby, Lucy had already spotted at least one taxidermied bird, frozen in mid-flight and affixed above a frosted glass door that led to the restrooms.

As she chewed on the end of her pen and watched the rain run in rivulets down the windowpane, she took just a minute to think about the past couple of months: Venice, with her new friends Bree and Carmen, and then St. Barts, where she'd gotten drunk and woken up mistakenly married to a younger man, but also where she and Nick had finally allowed themselves the space to let their relationship take a different direction.

Nick. Her cheeks felt warmer just remembering their first night together at the hotel. He'd pushed open the door of her room, and as they'd kissed hungrily, she'd tossed her purse aside, sending the contents rolling across the floor. And it had been comforting, too; finding that she and Nick were completely at ease with one another in bed had been a huge relief. Because of course—as with any woman approaching forty—Lucy had been let down in the past. Witty banter and casual friendship sometimes equaled zero chemistry behind closed doors, and an almost mutual dislike had on more than one occasion given way to an electric sizzle of passion with even the most unlikely of lovers.

But Nick had been perfect. His kisses were warm and tender, his hands searching and sure, his way with her both exciting and reassuring. She set her pen on the notepad and picked up her tea, watching as a woman fought with a royal blue umbrella in front of the bookstore across the street. She missed Nick. He'd been an easygoing companion on St. Barts and had talked her off the ledge after she'd had that horrific lapse in judgement that led her to trying on a wedding dress on a yacht and exchanging vows with a fireman ten years younger than her.

As if on cue, her phone chimed at her elbow and she set the teacup back on its saucer, smiling when she realized it was, in fact, Nick texting.

Hey, he said. *It's sunny and warm here and I've only had three customers in this morning asking if I could help them send an email to their grandkids. Do you think the snowbirds are flocking back from whence they came?*

Lucy chewed on the nail of her pinky finger as she read his words. The great migration of retirees to Florida usually reversed course right around Easter, so it seemed likely that in the very near future they'd be back to their regular population on Amelia Island.

Oh, Nicholas! Whatever will you do without your regulars dropping in to check their P.O. boxes for official Publishers Clearing House mail?

Almost instantly a photo came through of Hemingway, Nick's black lab, sitting in a patch of sunlight by the front door of The Carrier Pigeon, looking out at the parking lot.

I guess Hemmie and I will have to open a lemonade stand or something to bring in a few bucks.

Lucy smiled. *I miss you,* she typed, then re-read it a few times, her thumb hovering over the blue arrow before she sent it. Finally, with a quick burst of adrenaline and determination, she punched the arrow and sent her words across the ocean. There. It was done. She was being open and honest, even if it felt risky.

She put her phone down and picked up her tea again, taking a sip as the awning of the bakery across the street flapped wildly in the afternoon wind. The past couple of years had been a journey and a leap of faith, and in this particular moment, Lucy needed to take a breath and appreciate how far she'd come. Giving up her career as a forensic pathologist, leaving her hometown of Buffalo, moving south to Florida and attempting to care for her ailing mother long-distance, putting her painful divorce behind her and trying to trust again—it had all been hard, but she was making progress.

She never forgot the day her husband had come home from work and told her that he'd gotten a coworker pregnant, effectively bursting the bubble of innocence that Lucy had lived in up until that point. She'd believed in Jason—in their marriage and in their common goals —so much that she'd ignored the signs. She'd believed that the stress in their marriage was just her inability to conceive and that their jobs were mutually exhausting. Never once on her commute to work had she thought, "Hmm, maybe my husband is sleeping with his coworker who is seven years younger than him. Maybe he's fallen out of love with me. Maybe my life as I know it is about to end." But maybe she should have thought all those things. She definitely should have realized that something wasn't right.

With a sigh, she put the teacup down again and picked up her pen. There were still details to iron out for this visit to Edinburgh, and twenty-seven people would be arriving that evening at the hotel with its plaid curtains and stuffed fowl. Twenty-seven people were putting their trust in Lucy and hoping that she would have lined up all the best things for them to do on this trip to Scotland. And even more than the travel itself (which, admittedly, had been incredibly fun so far) it was this feeling, the feeling of being needed and counted on, that gave Lucy so much satisfaction. She loved it.

She reached for her notepad to jot down a few more things on her to-do list, but as she did, she glimpsed her phone screen. There, in a message bubble that sent a thrill from her scalp all the way to her toes, was a message from Nick that made her smile bloom like a sunrise:

I miss you more.

Chapter 3

April 12

London Heathrow Airport

Dane Demarco sat in a vinyl chair outside a sushi-to-go food stop in Heathrow, rubbing both temples as his wife motioned to him from the refrigerated case, holding up two identical looking packages of what had to be California rolls or tuna rolls. He gave her a tired thumbs-up.

This trip had been Olive's idea, and while he was glad to do whatever she wanted him to do at this point, there was no denying that traveling to another country with a group of strangers when he really should be back at home in San Diego working was a bit of an inconvenience.

"I got you a Sprite," Olive said, sitting in the chair next to Dane's. She hung the strap of her purse over one knee and handed him a can of soda and the plastic box that he could now see held a veggie roll. "Better for your health," Olive said without even glancing his way. "Too much mercury in tuna."

Dane inhaled and set the sushi on his lap as he cracked open his Sprite. "Thanks," he said, letting his eyes follow random travelers as they strolled up and down the concourse, some holding the hands of small children, some talking on cell phones, some pulling carry-on suitcases. Next to him, Olive carefully opened the lid to her sushi, pulled the paper wrapper off her wooden chopsticks, and tore the corner off a packet of soy sauce, which she proceeded to dribble all over her roll. It took everything in Dane's power not to beg her to stop.

"So," Olive said, popping a piece of salmon roll into her mouth and chewing with a hand held in front of her lips as she spoke. "We'll be in Scotland this evening. Are you excited?"

Dane took a big swig of his Sprite and grimaced as the carbonation went into his nostrils. "Yeah. Pretty stoked," he said, nodding and still ignoring his lunch.

"Here," Olive said, setting her own box on the empty seat next to hers. She reached over and picked up Dane's sushi. "Let me help you—"

"Olive," Dane said sharply. "I got it. I can open my own lunch when I want to eat it."

Olive let go of the box like it was on fire. "Sorry," she said, leaning over to pick up her sushi again. "Sorry."

Dane felt the instant flare of anger inside of him start to dim. It had been like this between them for some time: she would overcompensate with her kindness, and he would feel something in him snap as he watched his wife fixing little things or solving problems for him. And the worst part was that Olive absolutely, positively did not deserve his frustration. She'd done nothing wrong to earn his wrath in any corner of their lives.

"Ollie," Dane said, using the nickname he'd been calling her since they were twenty-three. "I didn't mean to be harsh. I'm just tired."

Olive didn't look at him. She shrugged and opened her own can of Diet Coke, taking a drink before she set it down at her feet and took another bite of sushi. "It's fine," she said softly.

Dane ran a hand through his hair and clenched his jaw. It was not fine, and they both knew it.

"Things have just been incredibly difficult," Dane said, pulling the lid off his sushi as a sort of concession to his wife for getting his lunch and for worrying about whether or not he was hungry in the first place. Olive had been looking after him for thirty years, and for that he owed her a debt of gratitude, not this asshole attitude he'd adopted in the past year or so.

"I know they have," Olive said, looking down into her tray of food. "I know they've been hard."

But did she really know? Did she understand how much he'd suffered, and could she really sympathize with him and not blame him for how their relationship had changed? There were just things they couldn't *talk* about—not if they wanted to wake up everyday in the same bed, say good morning to one another, and share a pot of coffee before work. If they wanted to maintain that status quo, then they needed to push certain things under the rug and just move on.

"Regardless," Dane went on, reaching out tentatively and putting a hand on his wife's knee. "I should never take out my feelings on you, Ollie. So please accept my apology."

Those seemed to be the magic words, as Olive turned the smile on Dane that he'd fallen in love with the day they met. In that moment, as they locked eyes and really and truly *looked* at one another, Dane could see it all: thirty years of family, of home, of love. He could see their four children and every Christmas, every birthday, every vacation they'd ever taken. He could see the pets they'd loved and lost, the weddings and funerals they'd attended, holding hands as they'd sat side by side in joy or grief. It was all there between them still: the love was as tangible as the chairs beneath them.

"Thanks for agreeing to come on this trip," Olive said, interlacing her fingers with Dane's and looking down shyly. "I wasn't sure if you would."

"Of course I would. I want to make things right between us. I owe you this, Ol." And that was true at least—he did owe her this trip to Scotland and so much more. For three decades she'd been a loyal and loving wife, and had not only worked full-time at the University of

San Diego running their alumni office, but she'd raised their four children and managed everyone's schedules and lives effortlessly.

Olive gave his hand a squeeze and let go, but before she did, he could see the tears that made her brown eyes glossy. Instead of letting them fall, she smiled again and reached for the Diet Coke she'd set on the ground.

Ollie, Dane thought, watching her. *My Ollie.* She'd always been his, and she always would be, even if she wasn't. There had been far too much between them to just pack it all up like holiday ornaments and shove their lives into a corner of the attic to be forgotten. He wanted to make this work, dammit, and he was committed to giving this trip his all. It didn't matter what it took: deep breathing, meditation, calming mantras; whatever it was, he'd do it.

"Flight 2918 to Edinburgh will begin boarding in approximately twenty minutes," said a female gate agent with a British accent. "Please prepare to board at Gate B23 for the flight to Edinburgh that departs at 15:42. Thank you."

Olive nodded at his lap to indicate that he should finish up whatever he wanted to eat, and then she put another bite of sushi into her own mouth and chewed with a half-smile on her face as people streamed by them, headed to destinations unknown.

* * *

The hotel in Edinburgh reminded Olive of a place they'd stayed on a road trip to Oregon when the kids were young. She and Dane had decided one summer that their children needed to see the entire west coast, so they'd driven a minivan full of pre-teens up Highway 101, stopping to see seals at the beach and to take photos in the Redwood Forest on their way to the Canadian border.

She sat now on the edge of the green corduroy duvet watching her husband unpack his suitcase into a polished wood dresser. He was only fifty-three—in fact, they both were—and yet he sometimes seemed older. More tired. Ever since things had gone wrong between them, he'd always seemed to her to be on the verge of a deep sigh.

"There's a Highland dance demonstration in the ballroom this evening during cocktail hour," Olive said, feeling hopeful that Dane's apology at the airport meant he'd be more willing to do new things. Instead of responding, he turned and picked up a stack of shirts from his suitcase and set them inside the drawer, which he closed firmly. "Do you think you'll feel up to going?"

Dane walked across the room and opened the minibar, crouching before it as he shuffled through the airplane-sized bottles of alcohol. He chose two small vodkas.

"Right now I feel like relaxing, Ol," he said, taking his bottles over to his side of the bed, kicking off his shoes, and twisting the cap on the first vodka, which he downed quickly with a puckered face. "I just need to chill out for an hour or so, okay?"

Olive pressed her lips together. "Okay." She tucked her short brown hair behind both ears. She'd cut it for this trip and he hadn't said a word, though she'd caught him looking at it with a distant frown, as if trying to remember how it had been before. "I think I'll go explore the hotel a little," she said, opening the closet and pulling out a yellow sweater that she'd already folded and placed on the shelf.

Dane patted the bed next to him and held out the unopened bottle of vodka. "You sure you don't want to join me?" he offered, though Olive felt it was a half-hearted invite.

She pulled the sweater on over her head and then ran her fingers through her hair. "No, you go ahead. I'll be back in a while."

As Olive closed the door to their hotel room behind her gently, she could hear the crack of the seal breaking as her husband twisted the cap off his second bottle of vodka.

Chapter 4

April 12
Edinburgh

Lucy weaved through the crowd that evening in the ballroom with a glass of wine in one hand that she refused to drink. She wanted the guests to see her as relaxed and as one of them, but she had no intention of kicking up her heels the way she'd done on St. Barts, partially because she was wary of her own ability to enjoy herself *too* much (hence the "waking up in a wedding gown next to a stranger" business), and partially because she felt differently without Nick at her side. It had always been her job and her job alone to run this travel group, but having him there had made it seem more like a vacation than a job, and this was most definitely her job, so she was prepared to treat it as such. At least on the first night.

The Highland dancers were dressed in plaid skirts with matching knee-high socks, and their jackets hit right at the waist, open to reveal matching vests beneath. Three men and three women leapt about on nimble feet, springing into the air as the bagpipe players did a rousing rendition of "Scotland the Brave." It was loud and festive, and as Lucy smiled at the guests she'd just met in the lobby, she noticed that they all watched with rapt attention and excited smiles.

Well, all except the three girls along the wall. Snow, Vanderbilt, and Filene (she couldn't have made these names up) were huddled near the bar, each holding a glass of champagne. Lucy knew they were taking their high school graduation trip together, and because they were in Scotland where the drinking age was eighteen, they were all old enough to imbibe a little. Still, they looked awkward and a little out of place, and she wondered why exactly they'd chosen this particular trip rather than, say, a cruise to the Bahamas or even a week in Disney World.

"Hi, ladies," Lucy said, stepping up to them. "How are things so far?"

Vanderbilt rubbed her glossy lips together and ran a through the ends of her long, highlighted hair. "So far so good," she said, looking at Lucy with hooded eyes. "This place is charming."

Snow, with a far more ample bust and hips than the other two, nodded along eagerly. "It's cool," she said, taking a swig of her champagne like she was drinking from a water bottle, which Lucy could more easily imagine her doing.

"We're really excited to be here," Filene added, holding out a hand to shake Lucy's. She had a chic brown bob and wore chunky, stylish glasses. "Thank you for letting us join the group." Filene looked like a young journalist, here to interview the other guests for a special on CNN. "Our parents said we could only come to Edinburgh if we were with a tour group."

Vanderbilt rolled her eyes and downed half her champagne in one gulp. "Lame," she said under her breath. "It's not like we're in Miami for spring break or something."

Snow giggled and as she did, her voluptuous breasts jiggled visibly from the top of her tight v-neck shirt, sending shockwaves of alarm through Lucy. When Filene's mother had called her directly to inquire about the young ladies coming on the trip without parental supervision, Lucy had envisioned three slightly nerdy girls who were dying to attend the Edinburgh Science Convention or to get photos taken with Captain America at the Comic Con that was taking place at the same time. What she had *not* bargained for was three young vixens who looked like they'd stepped off the set of *Mean Girls*, and who were now hungrily eyeing the young Scottish waiters circulating through the ball room with hors d'oeuvres and drinks.

"Scotland is definitely not Miami," Lucy agreed, almost putting her own glass of wine to her lips and taking a calming sip. Instead, she wrapped both hands around her glass and smiled at the girls. "But this should be a fun week. Anything you three are dying to do?"

A smirk spread across Vanderbilt's face as a waiter in his early twenties passed by in a kilt. "I'm dying to see what he's wearing under that skirt," she said, holding out her glass of champagne as she gestured at the handsome boy's retreating figure.

"Vandy!" Snow said with a snort.

Filene narrowed her eyes. "You can ho on your own time," she hissed at her friend. "Scotland is full of history and fascinating things and I want to see it all."

Lucy blinked a few times and looked around incredulously. Was this some sort of a put-on? She nearly laughed out loud at being in the middle of this conversation.

"Whatever," Vandy said, chugging the rest of her drink. "Oops, I'm out. Better go find more." She held up her empty glass and gave her friends a little smile before following the waiter.

Lucy waited a beat, then turned to Filene, who seemed to be the most adult of the trio. "So you'd like to take in some of the history of the country," she said, nodding and trying again.

"This year our history teacher did a whole unit on Scotland," Filene said, pushing her glasses up her nose in a way that seemed fashionable and not as nerdy as it would have looked on Lucy when she was eighteen.

"He was *super* hot," Snow added, leaning in close as if she were adding some sort of value to the conversation. "You have no idea. Filene had a huge crush on him."

Filene's eyes widened as she looked at Snow. "That's not all, Snow," she said archly. "He was also brilliant and a great scholar of all things Scottish."

Lucy folded; she put her wine glass to her mouth and took a sip—but just a small one. "What about the Comic Con? Any interest in that?"

Filene handed Snow her champagne and then opened her purse and dug around inside. "We could do that. I'm sure it would be fun," she said, sounding slightly bored. "Here," Filene pulled out her phone and unlocked it. She scrolled and swiped for a minute. "This is Mr. Hewes." Triumphantly, Filene held out the phone screen for Lucy to see, and sure enough, an extremely good-looking young man in horn-rimmed glasses sat on a low brick wall, one elbow on his knee as he smiled rakishly at the camera.

"Ah," Lucy said, giving in completely and taking another sip of her wine. "He looks nice."

"Nice?" Filene wrinkled her nose and pushed at her glasses again. "He's hot and now that I'm eighteen I want him to see me as a woman who can share his passions and interests."

Lucy couldn't see Filene for her passions and interests, but what she could now see was not a put-together, scholarly young woman, but a girl who probably traded in her contacts for stylish glasses to look older and smarter to the object of her desire. She saw three somewhat silly girls on the cusp of womanhood who weren't quite sure how to get there (*But did any of us actually know how?* Lucy thought. *Was there a roadmap?*), and what she saw most of all was a handful of work for herself over this next week. All three girls were eighteen, sure, but they were still under her care—was that right? Were they actually in her care? Technically their parents had signed off on this trip...regardless, they were a part of her tour group, and anything that happened to them happened to her, so she'd keep an extra watchful eye on these three just to appease herself.

"Hey," Vanderbilt said, walking back up to them breathlessly after chasing down the waiter. She held her phone up and made a little squeal like a happy kitten. "Got his number. And a selfie of us to post later so that Benton can see it. I don't even care if he's jealous—he can go suck it. For real."

"Listen," Lucy said, holding up a hand to pause this entire conversation. "I'm thrilled you ladies are with us, and I hope you have a fabulous time in Edinburgh. Of course I'm worried about you over-doing things. As people who can legally drink in this country but not at home, perhaps your tolerance is lower than you think."

Vanderbilt snorted and looked at her friends as if to say, *Is this chick out of her mind?*

"Lucy, it's not like we're new to drinking," Snow said gently, sounding like someone who was patiently breaking bad news to Grandma.

"Okay, but still," Lucy countered, her hand held up like a stop sign. "I'm sure your parents trust you to make wise choices, but ultimately you're here with The Holiday Adventure Club, and I want to make sure you ladies have fun, but also stay safe."

Filene, who had been holding her phone in her hand with Mr. Hewes still pulled up on the screen, locked the phone and dropped it into her purse. She gave Lucy a serious look through the lenses of her oversized glasses.

"Lucy," Filene said crisply. "We are fully grown adults. There is no way we could screw things up, because adults just make choices and then they go with it. When you're not a kid, no one questions that, right? You just do what you do, and everybody deals with it, no judgment."

It was possibly the funniest thing that Lucy had heard in, well, ever, but she stifled a laugh. "Uhhh," she said, squinting and turning to look at the Highland dancers while she pretended to think. "People definitely still judge, and most importantly, mistakes don't just go away." At this, she clamped her mouth shut; she could hear herself lecturing. "Anyway, you're going to have a great time." She smiled at the trio and started to back away. "Just let me know if there's anything I can do to help make things more fun."

As Lucy turned to find another guest to greet, she could see Vanderbilt and Snow openly gaping at her. "Okay, *Mom*," Snow hissed under her breath.

"Wow," Filene said, tossing her hair over one shoulder. "Just wow."

Lucy walked up to a man she'd seen during her welcome speech thirty minutes before, hoping to put a face with a name. Almost immediately, she put the girls out of her mind. They'd figure things out, and most likely they wouldn't get into any trouble in Edinburgh. After all, they were three eighteen year olds with credit cards and parents to call. They'd be fine.

"Hi," Lucy said, smiling widely and holding out a hand to the man she'd seen standing alone in the lobby as she'd greeted the tour group. "I'm Lucy Landish. Welcome to Edinburgh."

Chapter 5

April 13

Edinburgh

On their wedding day, Dane had looked like a movie star. Olive remembered seeing him standing at the altar, hands clasped in front of him, a look of wonder etched on his handsome face. He'd been a cross between a young Robert Redford with his sandy good looks and wry smile, and an impish Brad Pitt with his All-American blue eyes and cute features.

But now...now Dane was tired. He was distracted. He lived entirely inside of himself, and that smile wasn't quick to catch fire anymore. Ever since The Event—as Olive liked to think of it—had happened, her husband had become a shadow of his former self. And on most occasions he wasn't a friendly shadow. Through therapy Olive had learned not to blame herself, but it had been hard not to tally up her role in the way things had played out since The Event, hard not to wonder if she'd focused too much of herself on the children and their needs and not enough on Dane and his needs.

She watched him now, dressed in a navy blue v-neck sweater and jeans, hair thinning but still pushed to one side like a teenage boy who couldn't be bothered to tame it, and she couldn't help but smile.

Even after all the years, the kids, and, yes, even after The Event and its aftermath, Olive still loved him.

"Hey," she said, walking over to where he was standing on the sidewalk in front of the hotel. She'd excused herself for a last minute visit to the ladies' room in the lobby, promising to meet him outside.

"You ready?" Dane asked, his eyes cutting to her and then shifting back to the street again and the world around them.

He'd had more than the two bottles of vodka the night before, and she hadn't needed to check the wastebasket in the bathroom to figure it out. When Olive had returned from the Highland dance cocktail hour, Dane had been snoring loudly in his clothes on top of the bed, the smell of alcohol emanating from him with every breath.

"What do you think about Edinburgh Castle?" Olive slipped her hand into Dane's tentatively, hoping that he wouldn't just quickly crush her fingers and then let it go. To her surprise, he laced his fingers through hers and held on.

"Right now?"

"Sure. I asked at the front desk and we can get there by walking up the Royal Mile," she said, pointing to the east. "I heard there were lots of little attractions inside the castle and sometimes performers in period costume, so it sounded fun."

Dane kept his eyes trained forward as they were overtaken by a gaggle of school children in matching blue blazers and plaid skirts or khaki pants. The sound of their laughter and yelling trailed behind them and made Olive smile. It reminded her of April, Hunter, Jack, and Melody when they were little, and whenever the image of her beautiful children still in the midst of their youth came to mind it sent a wave of bittersweetness crashing through her.

"Remember—" she started to say at the same time Dane said: "I really need—"

Olive laughed. "You first."

Dane looked into her eyes for a split second and she hoped with all her might that he was going to say he needed her. He needed *them.* But instead he gave a quick smile and said: "I really need some more coffee."

It was a strange thing for Olive to get hung up on, but she stopped in her tracks, forcing Dane to stop to since they were still holding hands. "You need coffee, Dane? Really?"

He finally looked at her, eyebrows raised toward his receding hairline. "Yes?" he ventured.

"Well I need things too," Olive said, feeling a frown descend that would certainly not help her permanently furrowed brow. "I need..." She paused, unsure of how to articulate just what she needed.

Dane waited.

"I need..." Olive looked around wildly, hoping that the words would formulate so that she could finally tell her husband what she'd been longing for as they'd trudged through this bizarre, lonely time in their marriage, walking side-by-side, but not together as they'd tried repair all the damage that The Event had caused. Finally, a sense of calm settled over Olive like a blanket. She looked at Dane with steady eyes. "I need you to be happy again."

Something in Dane caved in as she watched his face, and Olive felt certain that he was going to pull her into his arms right there on the busy street as cars rushed by and people cut around them. In the best case scenario, he might even kiss her, completely oblivious to the rest of the world.

"Oh, Ollie," he said, his voice soft enough that only she could hear it. "What I really need to be happy right now is another cup of coffee."

Olive's face hardened just like her heart was doing in her chest and she dropped Dane's hand. "There's a tea room at the castle," she said coldly. "Let's get there and get you a coffee."

* * *

Edinburgh Castle was a short walk uphill from the Waverly train station. Olive and Dane mixed in with the crowds of tourists making the trek, though this time Olive walked far enough away from her husband that she didn't even attempt to hold his hand.

Inside, they bought two coffees, picked up an itinerary for a full morning and two headsets to listen to a guided tour of the castle, and without a word, Olive put hers on and started to wander. She'd find Dane later if she lost him. In fact, at that moment, she kind of hoped to lose him for a bit.

An hour and a half later, Olive had fully explored the "Fight for the Castle" exhibit as well as the Great Hall, so she wandered into the Crown Gift Shop and browsed through some of the crafts and souvenirs for sale. There were pieces of jewelry in gold and silver that were finely crafted with the faces of animals that lived in Scottish folklore, small pieces of pottery, and woven textiles made into throw pillows and heavy blankets. Olive wandered through the shop, touching it all and imagining which pieces she'd bring home to her children.

"I found you," Dane said, walking up behind her with his headset in one hand. "I think we lost each other somewhere in the Great Hall. It was pretty crowded."

"Mmhmm," Olive said, sounding noncommittal. She turned back to the sweater in her hands to admire the blend of reds and greens.

"For Hunter?" Dane nodded at the sweater. "He'd look good in that."

"He would," Olive said, putting it back. "But it's our first full day here, so I don't want to load up on gifts just yet. I need to see what else there is."

"Remember the earrings, Ol?"

Olive turned to look at him. Of course she remembered. They'd been in Palm Springs when the kids were small, and she'd seen a pair of gold hoop earrings in the window of a shop with little gems sprinkled all over them like confetti on a cake. Something about the way they sparkled made her feel like she'd be someone different if she wore them. Not a suburban mom from San Diego; not a woman in her late thirties; not someone who spent her evenings doing dishes and laundry. Instead, they would turn her into the kind of woman who went to outdoor music festivals. Someone who grew her hair long and cut bangs. The sort of mom who drank a glass of wine while she listened to music and tossed random ingredients into a pot on the stove for dinner.

But when Dane had offered to get them for her, she'd imagined the price tag and demurred. "No, no," she'd said, thinking of Jack needing braces, and of Melody's expensive ballet classes. "I wouldn't have anywhere to wear them anyway."

When they'd gotten back home, she'd lamented not getting the earrings more than once, but when Dane called the jewelry shop in Palm Springs they'd told him that the earrings had been sold and were a one-of-a-kind item. It was stupid, Olive knew, but missing out on buying those damn earrings had really rankled her. For years she convinced herself that if she'd purchased them, she'd be living an alternate reality. She'd be a different kind of woman. Maybe even the kind of woman who could have prevented The Event from taking her husband down in the first place.

She set the sweater back on the shelf and gave Dane a tight smile. "I do remember the earrings, but this is just a sweater for our adult son. Not the same thing at all."

They walked out of the shop and meandered over to the Whisky and Finest Food Shop, where Dane picked up two bottles of Edinburgh Castle's exclusive 10-year-old single malt, and then they found a table in the Tea Room and ordered an afternoon tea of smoked salmon tartlets, prosciutto di parma cups, a tray of tea sandwiches, and little cookies called Dundee Biscuits made of oats and topped with sliced almonds.

"Museums make me hungry," Dane said, popping the third salmon tartlet into his mouth.

"Yes, I know." Olive stirred a teaspoon of honey into her tea and chose a tiny finger sandwich from the tray, which she set delicately on her own small plate. "But most things make you hungry, Dane. Remember when we took the kids to Disneyland for the first time?"

Dane gave a hearty laugh and reached for one of the little muffin-sized cups made of baked prosciutto and filled with goat cheese. "I ate my way through that place."

Olive couldn't help it: she giggled as she took a bite of her egg and watercress sandwich. "Hot dogs, frozen bananas dipped in chocolate, popcorn."

"Beer, whipped pineapple ice cream, french fries."

"And the boys tried to keep up with you, but Hunter threw up all over Melody's new shoes after a spin on the tea cup ride."

"April," Dane said, holding a Dundee Biscuit in the air as he squinted his eyes, remembering that day. "They were April's shoes he threw up on. And I remember that because they had those sparkly initials on the sides."

"You're so right," Olive said, forgetting all about her sandwich as the image of that Disneyland debacle came back to her. "She had an AD on each shoe, and even though the letters were supposed to be for 'April Demarco,' Jack kept saying that it stood for 'Absolutely Disgusting' after the vomit incident, and April wouldn't stop crying."

Suddenly, they couldn't help themselves: laughter overtook them both and their shoulders shook. Tears sprang into Olive's eyes and she tried unsuccessfully to cover her open mouth with both hands to hold it all in.

"Ol," Dane said, hunched forward over his plate. His laughter shook the table and jostled the tea in their cups. "Oh my god, those kids. Aren't they something else?"

Without warning, Olive's laughing stopped. She felt a seriousness descend over her as she pictured all four of her children: April, Jack, Hunter, and Melody. They were all wonderful and so different from one another. Tears of a different kind threatened to fall.

"Yes," she said, her voice a hoarse whisper. "They are. They're magic."

Dane's face fell as he realized that Olive was about to cry, though this time not from laughter. "Oh, Ollie," he said, reaching across the table to take her hand. Around them, other tourists ordered tea sandwiches and snapped photos of the interior of the Tea Room for their Instagram accounts and to send to friends back home. "Those kids of ours *are* magic. And that's because of you."

Olive blinked a few times, unprepared as she was to hear compliments from Dane. "Oh, not just because of me," she demurred, picking up the napkin in her lap and using it to dab at her eyes as she glanced around from beneath her lashes, hoping that no one had caught the bizarre range of emotions that had swept over their table in the span of five minutes. "They're just amazing kids."

"Ol," Dane said, still holding her hand. He looked into her eyes, searching. There were things he clearly wanted to say, but instead of saying them, he continued to talk about their kids. "You've been the best mother I could have ever asked for to raise children with. You've loved and supported them, you have endless amounts of patience and understanding, and you knew when to have a light touch and when to be more serious. I would have never been able to do all of it without you."

Olive pulled her hand from his and smoothed her hair behind both ears. "That's true. You weren't home enough to do all of the child-rearing."

Dane winced. "Ouch."

"No," Olive said with a sigh. "I didn't mean to criticize. That's not what I meant."

"I know, I know. This is an argument we could have again and again: we both worked, but somehow you knew when to leave work at work and just be at home. I get it." A cloud descended over Dane's rugged face and he reached for another cookie. "It's a tale as old as time: Dad gets beat up for working his ass off to provide for family. Yadda yadda, etcetera, etcetera."

"That's not it, Dane." Olive frowned. "I just literally meant that I was there more than you were."

Dane's phone buzzed on the table and he picked it up, focusing on the screen as Olive tried to scramble and backtrack. They'd been having such a good time there for a moment...how could she get it back?

Dane pushed back his chair and tossed his napkin on the table carelessly. "I need to take this," he said, not looking at Olive. "It's Catherine."

Olive's heart sank and her shoulders dropped. Catherine. Of course. Without Catherine, they never would have had The Event. Without The Event, they never would have hit rock bottom. Without hitting rock bottom, they would still be Dane & Ollie, Ollie & Dane.

"Okay," Olive said, picking up another finger sandwich that she had no intention of eating. Dane had already walked through the front door of the Tea Room, leaving her there alone. "Okay," she said again, to no one in particular.

Chapter 6

April 13

Edinburgh

"And then when my brother was eight, I saved him from falling off a ladder and my mother was convinced that I had some sort of super powers," Edgar said, holding a beer in one hand and standing far too close to Lucy for her taste. She took a small step back. He honestly seemed like a nice man, but Edgar had the habit of leaning into a person's space while talking to them.

"Wow," Lucy said, reaching for the Diet Coke that she'd set on the tall bistro table at the pub down the street from the hotel. "You don't say."

"Yeah," Edgar went on, pushing a pair of thick, smudged glasses up his long nose and looking around at the other pub patrons. "I've saved a lot of animals, people, and whatnot."

"Whatnot?" Lucy took a drink of her soda and smiled politely. Edgar was clearly in his mid-fifties, and had come on the trip to Edinburgh alone with big plans to attend Comic Con. She'd already heard all about the costumes he'd packed.

Edgar shrugged. "Sure. And by whatnot I mean situations, mostly. Like one time I walked into a restaurant and a man was about

29

to propose to a woman, but he'd forgotten the ring. So I took off the one I was wearing—it was a silicone ring covered in Batman comic book pictures—and gave him that to use. He told me I saved the day." Edgar beamed and took a long pull on his beer, getting a dollop of foam on the end of his nose in the process.

"Well, that sounds pretty cool," Lucy said, nodding at him as she spotted Snow, Filene, and Vanderbilt slide into a booth at the other end of the pub. "How about animals?"

Edgar nearly vibrated with joy at being asked for more stories. Lucy could feel it coming off him and she took another small step back. There was no question that he was harmless, but he struck her as a tiny bit nutty and she didn't want him to get the wrong idea about her interest in his tales.

"When I was living in Manhattan in my twenties, I must have saved at least three cats from fire escapes, a bird trapped in a subway grate, and then there was the dog I rescued from being trampled by a horse-drawn carriage in Central Park," Edgar said, his eyes taking on a faraway look.

Lucy smiled and nodded as he talked, happy to listen. Weirdly, this was a part of the job she really liked, getting to know the travelers in her group. After so many years of spending her work days alone (for the most part) in a quiet morgue with humans who were no longer able to tell her stories about their lives, she kind of relished the bizarre situations and details people shared with her. Certainly she was intrigued—if a little worried—about what would happen in Edinburgh for her three eighteen-year-old charges, and she'd sensed some marital discord between the Demarcos, the couple joining them from San Diego. She'd fully expected them both to show up to cocktail hour the night before, but when she'd seen Mrs. Demarco standing there alone, looking downtrodden as she watched the Highland dancers, she'd wondered about their story and about what they wanted to experience on the trip.

"So then my neighbor was pounding on my door, and when I opened it, she had a bearded dragon in one hand, and a hammer in the other," Edgar was saying excitedly as Lucy tuned back in to hear what he was saying.

"Oh my gosh," she said, shaking her head in wonder. "That sounds crazy. And Edgar, I'm so sorry to cut you off, but I need to chat with those girls over there really quickly. Will you excuse me for just a moment?" To soften the blow of her abrupt departure, Lucy put one hand on Edgar's arm.

"Of course," he said, nodding kindly. "I'll tell you the rest later on." Edgar smiled at her, and Lucy could see in his eyes that he was truly a nice, if terribly lonely, man.

Across the pub, she approached the table of the three girls with what she hoped was a disarming smile.

"Ladies," Lucy said, glancing at the glasses of beer and the line of shots that they'd already ordered. "How's the day so far?"

Snow picked up her phone and started scrolling. This made Lucy feel like a high school teacher who was getting the cold shoulder.

"Today is great, Lucy," Filene said, giving her a winning smile as she twisted the ends of her hair around her fingers. "We're just having a little drink before we head over to check out the Comic Con."

"Oh!" Lucy said, feeling a burst of relief that they were going to be doing something wholesome for a few hours. "That's great. Edgar over there is really amped about the Comic Con as well."

Vanderbilt snorted audibly. "That guy is a mega nerd," she said, reaching for a shot glass. "Who gets 'amped' for a Comic Con?"

Snow laughed. "Right?"

Filene shot both of her friends a look before turning back to Lucy. "We're actually heading over to see if there's anyone cool to hang with."

"And also someone said Jason Momoa might be there dressed as Aquaman," Snow said, looking up from her phone. "Do you know what that means?"

"He'll be SHIRTLESS!" both Vanderbilt and Filene shouted, holding up their shot glasses and clinking them together. Two bearded, middle-aged men at the next table looked over to see what the commotion was.

Lucy couldn't help but laugh at their enthusiasm. She hadn't heard anything about Jason Momoa being at the Comic Con festival, but what did she know? And who was she to begrudge these younger women a little harmless fun?

"Okay, ladies, have a good time." Lucy smiled and turned to walk away, but before she went, she couldn't help adding an addendum: "Be safe!"

"Okay, Mom!" Snow said for the second time in twenty-four hours, only this time there was laughter in her voice rather than annoyance.

Lucy shook her head as she pushed open the heavy wooden door and stepped out onto the street. It was still early in the afternoon, and it looked to her like the girls might be completely sloshed within the hour. She reminded herself yet again that they weren't her full-time responsibility.

"Oh! Excuse me. I'm so sorry!" A woman walked straight into Lucy as she turned away from the pub. They collided and Lucy was pushed back by the force, causing her to bump into a parked bicycle, which toppled over. "Oh my goodness," the woman said, reaching for Lucy. "Are you okay?"

Lucy righted herself and secured her purse over her shoulder. "I'm fine," she said, straightening her short trench coat with both hands. "No harm, no foul."

"I was completely distracted—that was my fault." The woman standing before her, looking more apologetic than she needed to, was Mrs. Demarco. *Olive Demarco*, Lucy thought to herself. Olive was alone and looked completely distracted.

"Don't even give it another thought," Lucy said, holding out a hand. "I'm Lucy Landish. We haven't really gotten a chance to talk. I saw you last night at the cocktail hour, but when I finally got around the room after greeting some of the other guests, you were already gone."

Olive smiled. "I'm sorry. I should have introduced myself. Olive Demarco. My husband wasn't feeling well last night, so I just dropped in for a few minutes."

Lucy glanced around as she put her hands into the pockets of her coat. "Is your husband with you now? I'd love to meet him too."

"Dane? No," Olive said, plastering a smile on her face that Lucy could plainly see was several watts too bright. "He's off doing his own thing for a while. I thought I'd take a walk myself. I've been at Edinburgh Castle," she said, hooking a thumb over her shoulder to indicate which direction she'd come from.

"Ah," Lucy said, nodding. "And now? Are you off to somewhere in particular?"

Olive's smile dimmed. "No," she said, deflating slowly like a balloon that someone had punctured. "No. I have nowhere to go." Her eyes filled up with tears.

On impulse, Lucy reached out and took Olive's hand in her own. "Then come with me. I've been dying to sit down somewhere cozy and have a bowl of soup and I'd love the company."

"Really?" Olive's eyes widened. She was obviously at least a decade older than Lucy, and with her short haircut and lumpy, oversized cardigan, she looked like a mom who'd forgotten to pay attention to her looks as she'd raised her children.

"Yes, really. I heard there was a good restaurant within walking distance, and I'd love to hear more about you, Olive. So where are you from?"

Olive fell into step beside Lucy, buttoning her cardigan up to the collar to stave off the chilly spring weather. "San Diego," Olive said. "How about you?"

"Buffalo, originally," Lucy said, turning her shoulders sideways so that they could pass an older couple who were walking arm-in-arm on the sidewalk. "But I moved to this little beach town in Florida about a year and a half ago. It's called Amelia Island."

"I've been to Amelia!" Olive said, taking a couple of quick steps to keep up with Lucy, who was about six inches taller than her. "It's a very cute place."

"It is," Lucy agreed, stepping up to the restaurant that the girl at the front desk of their hotel had promised would give her a real taste of Edinburgh. She pulled open the door and let Olive walk in first.

Once they'd ordered two bowls of tattie soup ("It's potatoes, leek, carrots and celery in chicken broth," the waitress had told them patiently, guiding them towards something simple and hearty) and, at Olive's request, a bottle of white wine, Lucy sat back in the booth by the window and rested her hands in her lap.

"Ahh, this is nice," she said, glancing at the street outside as people dressed as superheroes and comic book characters passed by. "I mean," Lucy frowned, watching as a girl in a dog costume with a collar and leash held by a man in black latex walked past the window, "it's also a bit weird. But that's okay. Weird can be good, right?"

Olive picked up the glass of wine that the waitress had just poured for her. She'd also poured one for Lucy, then left the bottle on the table.

"I think I'm actually in the market for some normalcy at the moment," Olive said, taking a drink of the wine and letting it flood her body as she stretched her head from side to side. "I'm kind of at capacity for weirdness."

"Note to self," Lucy said, holding up an index finger. "Do not invite Olive to Comic Con to hang out with women dressed as dogs."

Olive laughed politely and downed about half of her wine in one go.

"Okay. So maybe I'll go first," Lucy said, feeling as if she already knew Olive. There was something about her that felt familiar, like an aunt who was both a good listener and someone who offered solid advice. It was unfair to cast her in this role given that they didn't actually know one another, but Lucy knew in her gut that anything they shared over a bottle of wine and a bowl of soup would stay there. "I started The Holiday Adventure Club and moved to Florida to escape a broken marriage and the responsibility that comes with my aging mother."

Olive took this in, nodding slowly as she did. "My husband and I have been married forever but now we're basically strangers who live together."

It was Lucy's turn to nod. The waitress materialized with their soup, set the bowls down, and left.

"I'd rather unpack your stuff, if you don't mind," Lucy said. "I could tell when we bumped into each other that you had a lot going on."

Olive put a spoon into her soup and stirred. "We've been miserable," she admitted, looking into the broth and watching the chunks of potato and carrot as they floated around the bowl. "I thought this trip would bring us closer together, but so far all he's done is drink, grit his teeth, and take a phone call that ruined our morning."

Lucy put a spoonful of soup into her mouth and watched Olive. She wanted to ask questions, but she also wanted the other woman to keep talking.

"See, this thing happened a couple of years ago that really changed everything. Almost overnight, Dane went from being this open, funny, caring guy to a person who shut down completely." Lucy picked up the bottle of wine and topped off Olive's glass. "The kids and I didn't think he would ever disappear on us, but somehow he did—without going anywhere." She lifted her wine glass and looked out the window at the street. "God, he'd kill me if he knew I was telling all of this to a stranger," she said. "But I can't talk about any of this with the kids, and I certainly can't tell my girlfriends, you know, 'Hey, my husband went off the deep end, shut me out, lost his job after twenty-five years, and sometimes I don't even know who he is anymore.' That kind of gossip would definitely make the rounds in our circle."

"I hear you," Lucy said. "Sometimes it's impossible to be totally honest with the people closest to you. It just doesn't work."

"Right? You have to keep up a façade." Olive knocked back

another big gulp of wine. "But it's the façade that kills you. It crushes your spirit. Makes you want to go crazy and become someone else."

Lucy thought about the way she'd felt when Jason had upended their life together. Yeah, it had crushed her spirit a little. And yeah, the idea of staying in Buffalo and doing the same thing, day in and day out, taking care of her mom's bills and running to the store for her all the time had made her feel like going crazy. So she'd done exactly what Olive was saying: she'd run away and become someone else. This was all totally relatable to Lucy.

"And coming to Edinburgh was your way of getting away and going at least a little crazy?" Lucy took another spoonful of her soup.

Olive smiled guiltily and motioned to herself. "Yeah. I'm sure you can tell just by looking at me that I'm not particularly wild and impetuous. Safe haircut. Boring makeup. Simple sweater and jeans."

"Oh, I don't know," Lucy said, picking up her own glass of wine as she considered Olive. "You look happy with who you are. Comfortable. I think there's something to be said for that."

"Thank you for saying so. But mostly I think it's pretty boring. I feel like Dane has completely lost interest in me and I need to reinvent myself to get his attention back."

"I actually have some experience with a marriage that hit the skids. I had no idea I'd lost his attention until he came home one day and admitted to an affair with a coworker. But he only told me about it because she was pregnant. So," Lucy said, dropping her voice, "I do know what it's like to be in your shoes and to have to deal with the aftermath of an affair. And I admire you for wanting to fix things—I think that's really honorable."

"Oh!" Olive put a hand to her chest and her spoon clattered in her bowl. "Oh—no. I'm sorry, Lucy, I didn't mean to let you believe that Dane had an affair. Things are bad, but not because of anything like that."

Lucy leaned back in the booth, waiting to hear more.

"See, there was this thing that happened. In my mind, I call it The Event, but really it was more of a revelation that sent him spiraling out of control." Olive leaned forward, eyes flashing. This was the most animated Lucy had seen her, and while it was possibly from the wine she was drinking at a fairly rapid clip, it was clearly also from the passion she still felt about her marriage.

"Go on," Lucy said, picking up her glass again and holding it as she kept her eyes on Olive's face.

"Well, it all started one Thanksgiving when his sister Catherine came to visit..."

Chapter 7

April 14

Edinburgh

Jupiter Artland was essentially a huge art museum set on 120 acres of woodland outside the city. Lucy trekked there along with ten of her guests the next day, admiring the grounds of the nineteenth century Bonnington House and the giant landforms that were surrounded by four lakes. Each landform had been shaped into whimsical swirls of golf course green grass, and the lakes were glassy and smooth.

Almost immediately, the group of ten moved en masse to start a guided tour, but Lucy found a quiet spot near a swimming pool that was tiled with a rainbow of colors in long strips and swirls that mimicked the grassy knolls. Since it was April and not terribly warm, no one lingered at the pool to dip a toe in, so Lucy found a bench and sat near a miniature dome covered in reflective glass that reminded her of the one at Epcot in Disney World.

She'd spent a good part of the evening before talking to Olive and listening to her story, and while she'd been more than happy to do so, it had also been exhausting and she'd gone right back to the hotel and slept the sleep of the dead.

Now, at ten o'clock in the morning and after breakfast and two strong cups of coffee, she was ready to attend to her own personal business.

She had three messages: one from Nick, one from her aunt Sharon, and one from Dev. Without stopping to analyze the choice, she opened Dev's message first.

Hey, world traveler. How goes it? Feels like you were barely home before you turned around and left again, and I wanted to check in on how many people signed up for this one. Did our plan to advertise in Comic Con Facebook groups work? Take it easy.

Lucy read it twice and then looked up, scanning the grounds around her. In the distance, she could see a huge high-heeled shoe made out of metal discs, and the stately manor itself, holding court on the grounds like a very proper nanny overseeing a bunch of wild children. The art installations made it feel like someone had overturned a box of giant toys and spilled them all over the property. As she watched, Lucy could see a family posing for photos in front of the high-heeled shoe.

So, Dev is still talking to me. Okay. But of course he was. It wasn't as though they'd started some sort of torrid romance that had been interrupted by Nick or anything. They'd gone to one concert and had flirted awkwardly and mildly for the past year or so. No big deal. Lucy looked back at the phone screen and started tapping out a message.

I've got a good group here. 27 people. I think a few of them signed up from the Facebook groups, and one of them seems to believe he's actually a superhero, so there's that. How are things?

She second-guessed the "how are things?" after sending the message, but only for a split second. It wasn't like she and Nick were in some high school relationship where neither of them were allowed to have other friends, right? She closed Dev's message and moved on to Aunt Sharon's.

Hi, hon. Your mom has been restless the past couple of days and is asking for your dad. What do I do? Hope Scotland is treating you well.

If you see Mel Gibson in a kilt, bring him home for me! Love, Aunt Sharon

Lucy smiled. It was cute how her aunt felt the need to sign the text like an email, but it was decidedly un-cute that her mother was confused enough to be asking for her father. She needed to shut that down immediately.

Hi, Aunt Sharon! Scotland is gorgeous. A bit overcast and chilly, but truly beautiful. I love it. As for my mom, I'm sorry to hear that she's restless, but NO, do not let her reach out to my dad in any way. I haven't talked to him in three years and I'm not even sure whether my mom has spoken to him in the last decade. I think that would be bad. Thank you for looking after her and I'll send pictures! xo

Lucy sighed and closed her eyes, breathing in the clean, grassy air and feeling the cool Scottish breeze on her face. She hadn't regretted leaving Buffalo for a single second since driving away, but her mother complicated things—a lot. Her feelings and guilt over being away were sometimes immense, but her relief at the distance between her and her old life was tangible. She opened her eyes and looked at her phone again.

Hey, Nick said. *I miss you. Can we FaceTime later? Hemingway wants to see you—he said he thinks he forgot what you look like. Crazy dog.* He followed this up with an emoji of a panting dog and one of a little man shrugging his shoulders and Lucy smiled.

Of course we can! I miss you too—both of you. I'm at Jupiter Artland right now with ten of the travelers and it's really weird and cool. Check out this pool I'm sitting next to while I message you, and I'll try to call you around noon your time.

Lucy turned her phone sideways to get a good panoramic shot of the colorful pool, the verdant grounds, the steely gray clouds that hung along the horizon, and the very proper looking Bonnington House in the distance, then she sent it to Nick and closed her phone, dropping it into her shoulder bag before she stood up and stretched.

Her group was walking across the grass as she made her way toward the giant main house. She lifted a hand and waved. Edgar waved back excitedly and stayed behind for a moment, waiting for Lucy to catch up. She couldn't help but notice that he wore a Superman t-shirt underneath his denim jacket, the appliqué on the chest stretched tight and slightly faded.

"You joining us, boss?" Edgar asked with a friendly smile as Lucy approached the group.

"I think so." She pulled her jacket tighter against the cool weather and fell into step with them. "Pretty interesting place, huh?"

Edgar stopped walking. His face went dark. "Wait," he said. "Uh uh."

"Uh uh, what?" Lucy stopped walking and stared at him. "You okay?" He genuinely did not look okay, but she was hopeful that it was just heartburn or something. "Edgar?"

"Give me a second, please," Edgar said, holding up a hand. Suddenly, he turned and broke into a dead sprint across the manicured lawn, jean jacket flapping as he ran, his middle-aged body lumbering as quickly as Lucy had seen a man his age run.

"Edgar?" she called lamely. But he was already headed in the direction Lucy had just come from.

At that point, at least half of their group realized that there was some commotion and everyone had stopped walking and turned to watch. Lucy felt helpless, but also like she needed to see what he was doing.

"Edgar?" she called again, this time taking strides to follow him.

Through the bushes that surrounded the rainbow-tiled pool, Lucy could hear Edgar's voice. "It's okay, I got you," he said, repeating himself two more times as the full pool area came into view for Lucy. She didn't realize it, but the other nine members of their group were right behind her and one of the women shouted, "Oh!" as she came upon the scene, nearly bumping into Lucy from behind.

Edgar was on his hands and knees, soaking wet, doing CPR on an elderly man in a tweed jacket. Lucy sprang into action, the doctor in her ready to help in any way she could as she dropped her purse and fell to her knees beside Edgar and the man.

Between breaths, Edgar lifted his head and looked in the direction of all the spectators. "Get help," he said, then went back to work.

Two teenage boys had been attracted by all the action and right away, one of them broke away and fell into a flat-out run, his loping strides so different from Edgar's labored run. It was more gazelle than elephant as Lucy watched him cover the grounds between the pool and the manor house in record time.

Within seconds, the old man sputtered and a gurgle of water shot from his mouth. He coughed and squeezed his eyes shut, but Edgar forced him into a sitting position and then held him upright as Lucy looked into his face to assess whether he was turning blue or would need any reassurance about where he was and what was going on. She took his hand in hers gently as he came to.

"Got you, old chap," Edgar said, rubbing the older man's back with slow circles and talking to him quietly. "You're alright."

By the time the medics arrived to take the man away on a stretcher, quite a crowd had gathered. Lucy still couldn't fathom how Edgar had known to set off running and to go directly to the pool, but he was busy talking to other people and so she didn't ask.

The rest of the afternoon had a slightly surreal quality, and the group wandered together through the woods, which was filled with various art installations and sculptures that somehow were both totally incongruous with the forest and also totally at home there. Lucy snapped pictures of giant blown glass flowers in a riot of colors, an abandoned baby doll made to look like an alien on a mossy beds at the base of a tree, and a fake fairytale shop built amongst the trees where everything inside was upside down. She sent them all to Nick and then followed the group, watching as people took turns walking alongside Edgar. He had a newfound popularity amongst his travel companions and was enjoying every minute of it, as far as Lucy could tell.

Back at the hotel, Lucy took off her coat and chose the table by the window where she'd had tea her first day. She ordered coffee and a plate of cookies and then leaned back with a sigh.

"May I join you?" Edgar asked, having finished a conversation with a couple from Dallas who'd spent the day at the Edinburgh Science Festival rather than joining them at Jupiter Artland.

Lucy motioned at the high-backed chair across from hers. "I just ordered coffee. I need an infusion of caffeine," she said. "We've got a whole pot coming, so feel free to partake."

"Don't mind if I do," Edgar said, taking off the windbreaker that the people at Jupiter Artland had given him to wear in place of his wet denim jacket. His Superman t-shirt had long since dried, and he'd managed to only get the knees of his jeans wet as he'd knelt next to the pool to save the elderly man.

"I have to know, Edgar," Lucy said right away, "how you knew to run to the pool. Most people have instincts about things—gut feelings, if you will—but that sort of deep knowing is one I've never encountered myself."

Edgar crossed one knee over the other and smiled placidly. "I told you, Lucy, I'm a saver. I can save anyone, anywhere, at any time."

Lucy nodded slowly, waiting for the woman in the plaid skirt who'd served her tea the first day to set down a tray of coffee, cream, and cookies. "Thank you," she said absentmindedly, still focused on Edgar.

"I have a long track record," he said, reaching for a cookie before Lucy could even offer. "It goes back to childhood."

"Right, the animals and stuff." Lucy reached for the carafe of coffee and poured some for both herself and for Edgar, as the woman had kindly brought two cups. "But how do you *know* something needs to be saved? It can't just be a case of you being in the right place at the right time." She shook her head, pouring a thin ribbon of cream into her cup and stirring it with a spoon. "We weren't even within shouting distance of the pool today, and there was no one there to yell for help anyway, just the guy who'd fallen in."

Edgar scratched his head. "Well, that's the mystery, isn't it? You're a doctor," he said, his smile creasing the corners of his eyes.

"You must know that there are human mysteries that simply can't be solved."

Lucy frowned and broke a cookie in half before she dunked it in her coffee and took a bite. She chewed thoughtfully. "Right, that's true...to a certain extent. But humans aren't entirely enigmatic. Our physical functions are magical, yes, but they can also be explained by science."

"And how about our metaphysical functions?" Edgar took another cookie.

Lucy acquiesced by lifting her coffee cup with both hands and letting her eyes slide to the window where she again watched the passerby mingling with traffic and attempting to share the sidewalk, just as she'd done on that first rainy day in Edinburgh.

"True," she said, sipping the hot coffee. "There are things we just can't—or don't yet—know. And I'm a believer in such things, though many of my colleagues are not." It struck her as she said this that she was referring to her former colleagues, which felt weird. She sat with that for a moment. "Anyway, what sort of alarm goes off inside of you? Or how do you become aware of what's going on and who needs assistance?" she asked, looking directly into Edgar's eyes. She felt compelled to know now that she'd seen him in action and could no longer simply write him off as some kooky guy in a pub talking about saving birds and bunny rabbits.

Edgar shrugged. "I start to feel a warmth creeping over my skin," he said, using his hands to mime a scratching sensation on his arms. "And sometimes I stop being able to hear what's going on right in front of me. Instead, I hear a roaring sound like the ocean and I get pushed in a certain direction. So then I just go."

"Pushed? Like by a hand?"

"I'm not sure, to be perfectly honest. Like today, I felt something push me toward that pool. I knew I'd find someone or something who needed my help. And sure enough, there was a guy floating facedown at the edge of the pool."

Lucy had felt that perhaps he'd had some sort of cardiac event or even a stroke standing there alone, but she'd leave that up to the doctors treating him; her only concern now was how Edgar had known to go to him.

"Wow," Lucy said, shaking her head. "I'm amazed. And impressed. This is all so fascinating to me."

"It's just my life," Edgar said, pouring himself more coffee. "It always has been."

Just then, Snow, Filene, and Vanderbilt walked through the lobby. To Lucy, they were almost a visible cloud of perfume, dry shampoo, fruity lipgloss, and body lotion.

Edgar glanced at them pensively. "Now take this situation," he said, biting into his fourth cookie. "I'm a fifty-four-year-old man, and I know those girls are going to find trouble wherever they go, but it would be weird if I followed them to make sure they were okay."

"This is true," Lucy agreed. "It would be weird, but they do seem destined for some sort of trouble." She wasn't thinking of potential drowning or anything, more like flirting with the wrong guys.

"It's a shame because I'd really like to be there to push one of them out of the way of a bus while she's busy checking her own reflection in a shop window."

Lucy laughed; the chances were extremely high that this could actually happen.

"I'll keep my fingers crossed that they stay away from danger," Lucy said, picking up a cookie herself. "But if they end up in a sticky situation, I'll hope that EdgarMan is there to save the day." She winked at him.

Edgar chuckled. "You'd be surprised at how many times I've been called that in my life."

Chapter 8

April 15

Edinburgh

The church bells were ringing all over the city and Olive was dressed in a flowered skirt and a lilac blazer with matching shoes. It had seemed like the perfect Easter outfit when she'd packed it back in San Diego, but now that she was looking at her reflection in the mirror of the hotel room, she realized how much she looked like Queen Elizabeth: dowdy and too proper. With a sigh of resignation, she fluffed her short brown hair a little and took off the silk scarf she was wearing, tossing it on the foot of the bed. There, at least that loosened her up a little.

"You look nice," Dane said, coming out of the bathroom in his shirt and tie. He'd just shaved, and he smelled clean and soapy, the way Olive preferred him.

"Thank you. So do you." Things were lukewarm between them, but on the whole, genial and non-confrontational, which Olive preferred for Easter.

Dane slipped into his jacket while Olive put a few things into her purse, and then they were off, joining the foot traffic of Edinburgh as people walked to church in bright hats and smart clothes, or to brunch in jeans and sweaters. The night before, Olive had selected a ten o'clock service at Sacred Heart to attend, and Dane hadn't argued with her but had extracted a promise to have lunch out and to do more sightseeing after.

The service was completely full, and Olive spent the entire time reveling in the ceremony of it, enjoying the priest's thick Scottish accent, and watching the people around her. Of course there were fanciful hats on the women, lots of white gloves, and children dressed and spit-polished for the occasion, but there were also men with their hands folded, looking quiet and contemplative, and she liked that. It wasn't often in this world that you went somewhere anymore and a whole roomful of people kept their phones put away and all looked at the same thing, listening and thinking and just *being*. Olive loved it.

After the service, Olive made good on her promise and they went back to the hotel to quickly change into jeans and shoes for walking, then they made their way to Victoria Street, which was known as a haven for foodies and people who love little boutiques.

Dane had a handful of shops he wanted to go into, including one that sold tweed jackets and another that specialized in single malt whisky, but first he steered Olive to Maison Bleue for lunch, where, shockingly he already had a reservation under his name. The outside of the restaurant was a bright, shocking blue, and through the windows, Olive could see that it was a combination of French and some kind of farm-chic.

"Dane!" Olive said in surprise, looking at her husband with new eyes. She'd watched him carefully during the Easter church service, and while he'd sometimes seemed faraway, he'd also never felt closer, sitting there next to her with his arm brushing hers, the heat of his familiar body emanating off of him in waves. "I didn't know you made us a reservation."

"Of course," he said, seeming more like the old Dane she'd married than he had in a very long time. "It's Easter and I wanted to take you somewhere nice."

The hostess led them to a rustic, rough wooden table with two mismatched chairs. The walls were painted a deep, matte blue, and each of the high-backed booths around the restaurant were different jewel tones and made of tufted velvet.

"Thank you," Olive said, accepting a menu.

The music was French and the other diners looked relaxed and happy to be out for the holiday. A couple in the corner had an Irish Setter sitting beneath their table, something Olive always took issue with at home, though in this setting the dog looked totally at ease. A fireplace on one side of the restaurant was filled with wood and crackling flames. Something about the whole scene just felt cozy and filled Olive with a sense of well-being and goodwill.

"I'm just amazed that you made reservations in advance. You always used to do that for holidays, but...it's been a while," she said, picking up her menu and focusing on it so that she didn't have to look directly at her husband.

Dane was silent for a beat too long, so Olive set the menu on the table and glanced up at him. He was watching her intently. "I am trying, Ol. I promise I am."

Olive gave him a half-smile and looked down at the thick white linen menu.

"Could we please start with the oeuf cocotte," Dane said to their waitress when she reappeared. Olive scanned the list of starters and quickly read that this was a poached egg in a creamy blue cheese fondue with croutons and fries. Her stomach growled audibly; they'd forgone breakfast in favor of church. Other than a cup of coffee that Dane had gone to grab in the lobby that morning, all she'd eaten since dinner the night before was a pillow mint.

"And then I think we'll share a wild mushroom risotto," Dane went on, eyes flickering to his wife's face to confirm that he should keep ordering for them both, something he'd done when they'd first dated and that she loved. She gave him a quick nod. "And we'll also do the aubergine tower," (*roasted vegetables with mozzarella and a sweet pepper dressing*, Olive read) "and an order of the haggis balls, because when in Rome," Dane added, smiling at Olive.

The waitress smiled at them. "Daring, you Americans. Do I need to describe haggis at all before bringing it, just so you're sure?"

"Oh, please don't," Olive said, waving a hand to stop her from going on. "I'll nix the whole thing if you do."

"Wouldn't be the first time, lass," the waitress said with a wink.

"And could we please start with a bottle of the Sauvignon Blanc —the French one whose name I won't dare to butcher with my American accent," Dane said, handing over their menus.

"Ah, the 2018 Ladoucette Pouilly-Fume." Their waitress nodded knowingly as she tucked their menus under one arm. "That will be lovely with the risotto. Wonderful choice."

When they were alone again, Dane folded his hands on the table and looked at the fire. "So," he said. "I was thinking—"

At the same time, Olive started to speak: "I hope you—"

They both laughed. "You first," Dane said, holding out a hand to indicate that she should speak.

"I was just going to say that I hope you enjoyed the service as much as I did. I know we've only ever been holiday churchgoers, but I always love the feeling of peace I get when I'm sitting in a church with a whole group of people who are just breathing and taking in the words of a priest. That, and the collective joy we share when we all sing."

Dane looked taken aback. "Wow. I wasn't going to say anything that deep—I just thought we might do some shopping after lunch and hit that store we passed where they sell all the Harry Potter memorabilia so we can get a few things for Jack. He's always been such a fan."

Olive laughed. "True, he has."

"But yes," Dane said, circling back to her comment. "I did enjoy it. You know how hard it is to shut off the buzzing in your brain and to put work aside, but somehow you just do when you're in a holy place on a day when you know you should. So yes, I felt the same sense of peace that you did. In fact, it was probably the first time since we landed here that I've gone for any stretch of time not worrying about answering emails or taking calls."

Olive leaned back as the restaurant's sommelier arrived with their Sauvignon Blanc, uncorked it, and poured two glasses. He waited as they each took a sip and then nodded their approval, then set the bottle on their table and disappeared.

"I've never found it as difficult as you to put work aside, but I do love hearing that at least *something* stills that constant need to stay on top of things. FOMO, I think they call it."

"What's FOMO?" Dane frowned.

"Fear of Missing Out."

"Ah. Right. And it does feel like that. Like, I'm going to pick up my phone and find that I've missed an important call or have neglected my job altogether. I don't know why I care so much. This isn't even my career of choice," he added sadly.

Olive remained quiet, her hand on the stem of her wine glass as she watched the flicker of the fire reflected in the glass. Outside, the sky was still that gray flannel that she'd already come to associate with Edinburgh; it made the city seem like something out of a 19th century British novel.

"I guess I care because I know that I'm barely hanging on," Dane said quietly, staring into his own glass as if the wine itself might hold the answer to all of his questions and solve all his troubles.

"Dane, that's not true. You're doing so much better."

"Yeah," he said, looking defeated. "I'm okay. Talking to that gal has helped."

By "that gal," Olive knew he meant the therapist that his company's HR department had directed him to speak to. Convincing a man in his 50s that telling all his troubles to a stranger was the answer to his problems was a tough sell, but at the behest of his immediate boss (and as a requirement of his continued employment there) he'd done it.

"I'm glad to hear that," Olive said carefully. She'd seen some improvements at home after Dane had started meeting with his therapist twice a week, but she'd made sure not to ask too many questions about it or to let on that she was thrilled he was getting help.

"Well, it's nice to hear that I'm not crazy," he said, cutting his eyes at the tables closest to them to make sure that no one could overhear their conversation. "But it's also good to have someone give me guidance on how to keep it all together. Because for a while I really wasn't keeping it all together."

Understatement of the century, Olive thought, but didn't say out loud. She nodded and took a sip of her wine to make it clear that she was listening and not speaking.

"Having Catherine turn my world inside out like that really did a number on my head, Ollie. I felt like I wasn't even myself anymore. It was like all the things I thought were mine: you, the kids, my career, just all of it—maybe were just figments of my imagination. Can you understand that?"

"I've really tried to, Dane. I've done my best to understand and to be here for you," Olive said, the words spilling out before she could stop them. She set her wine down and looked at him intently. "I never wanted you to feel alone, or like you couldn't handle life. And maybe this all just happened at the worst time, which would be midlife, when things are hard anyway, but maybe it would have always thrown you for a loop. I don't know. But I am thrilled that you're getting help, and that work is going okay, and that—"

Dane held up a hand to stop the onslaught of words. "Thank you, Olive," he said firmly. "I'm a lucky man to have your support, but I'm not ready to talk about all of it here, over lunch."

Olive clammed up, which was fine, as the waitress had returned with their starter and then picked up the wine bottle and topped off both of their glasses. Olive waited until they were alone again, and in the meantime, the logs on the fire across the room cracked loudly, startling the Irish Setter, who lifted his head, ears perked.

"Dane," Olive started, choosing her words. "If things are going to go forward for us, and believe me, I've given a lot of consideration to whether that's even possible, then I need to be a part of your process." She leaned across the table so that she could drop her voice and still be heard. "I don't need to go to therapy with you, and I don't need you to tell me everything—or anything—that happens there, but I need to know how you're doing. This whole thing where you hold me at arm's length and then sometimes you snap at me, or sometimes when I least expect it, you're kind and considerate, is really hard to maintain. You keep me walking on eggshells all the time and that's impossible for me."

Dane nodded, eyes downcast. "I know, and I'm sorry. But you can't imagine how difficult it was to find out all the things I did."

"I can though," Olive said, her voice firm and clear. She sat back in her chair. "I can because I was there. I watched you unfold and come apart, and I've watched you try to put yourself back together. But you know what it's doing to me?"

"Olive," Dane said with warning in his voice. "Please. Lower your voice."

Olive shook her head vehemently. "No. Not this time. You need to hear this," she said, jabbing a finger at the table with each word. "While you're slowly putting yourself back together, you're taking me apart. Who am I, Dane? Who am I anymore? Has it ever occurred to you that maybe I'm someone facing my own midlife crisis? My own wonderings about who I am and where I'm going, and my own sorrows over not having accomplished all that I wanted to?" Olive pushed back her chair and stood up, nearly knocking over her wine in the process. "I'm tired of constantly worrying whether something I say or do will upset you, and I'm tired of waiting to see how you'll treat me today. So Dane, either you treat me like your loving wife *every day*, or you treat me like a stranger and we'll go our separate ways. I'm done with being all the king's horses and all the king's men, trying every damn day to put Humpty together again."

For a moment, Dane looked as though he'd been slapped. But as he stared at his clearly very angry wife, a smile spread across his face and he gave a loud, hearty laugh. "Humpty? Olive!" He laughed again, looking at her with wonder.

But Olive couldn't take this change of mood—not again, not now —and it took everything in her not to stamp her foot angrily in frustration. He was *always* like this: one minute morose and droopy like a total Eeyore, the next minute laughing, and before she knew it, snappy and cold again. And she was tired of it.

Olive grabbed her purse and coat from the seat next to hers. "Enjoy your lunch, Dane," she said, picking up her glass of wine and draining it in one go—a move entirely uncharacteristic of her, but it felt good. In fact, it felt amazing. She set the glass down and turned on her heel before her husband could say a word to stop her.

On the walk back to the hotel, Olive entertained every idea she could come up with: pack her things and fly back home without Dane? Call one of her daughters and finally take them up on the offer to come and visit? Melody had a spare room in her little bungalow in Santa Barbara, and April, who was sharing an apartment with a traveling nurse in San Francisco, was almost always alone and would be thrilled to see her mother. Or at least Olive thought she might. Her pace slowed and she really considered it: would her daughters want their mom invading their lives, or was that just an offer they put out there knowing that she'd never take it? What woman in her late twenties really and truly hoped that her mother would show up with a packed bag and set up camp?

Olive's phone rang as she walked and when she pulled it out of her purse, she saw that it was Dane. She rejected the call and shoved the phone back in her bag. She kept walking.

It served him right, always acting like she was a piece of furniture that he hadn't quite gotten into the right place. When would he ever learn? A man didn't need to share every thought that went through his head, but seriously—was it too much to ask to get a little update on how her own husband was feeling? Could he possibly let her know where things stood without being standoffish, drinking too much, or snapping and then apologizing for it?

It was a spur of the moment decision for sure, but Olive was walking down the street where the Comic Con was taking place, and when she saw a sign advertising tickets she walked right up to the window and bought one. And why not? She was essentially living in a fantasy world anyway, trying to be a superhero herself on a daily basis. She got up, went to work, made sure to answer every text and call from her four children, checked in on her own aging parents, cooked dinner, and waited anxiously each day to see how Dane was feeling. Was she expected to have x-ray vision? Some sort of super-human insight?

The boy in the ticket booth slid her a wristband and her credit card, and Olive slipped the band on without hesitation. She literally had no idea what happened at a Comic Con, but based on the people streaming in and out wearing what were essentially Halloween costumes, she guessed it had something to do with play-acting. Or maybe it was like attending a showing of *The Rocky Horror Picture Show*, which she'd done a time or two as a teenager.

Inside the building, Olive encountered more superheroes than she could count. Her son Jack had been deeply into Marvel comics as a young boy, so she knew some of the characters she was seeing, but the intricacy of the costumes was amazing. There were teenage girls and young women in extremely high boots that laced up to the knee, stage makeup, and colorful wigs; men wearing tight spandex body-suits and capes with masks; and people so deeply shrouded in costumes with full heads and gloves that she couldn't even tell if they were male or female.

"Take a picture with you, miss?" Spiderman stopped in front of Olive and did a theatrical pose with both hands outstretched as if he were throwing spiderwebs from each finger.

Olive laughed. "Oh! No thank you. Maybe later," she added, smiling kindly and stepping around him.

The concourse of the convention center was lined with curtained off booths, and in each booth was someone worth stopping to see: a comic book illustrator with stacks of his own self-published comics that he was autographing for fans (she bought one for Jack); a group of beautiful and tough-looking girls dressed up like some sort of dolls come to life and armed with (fake) weaponry; anime characters; and every middle-of-the-road superhero Olive could imagine. After stopping to chat with a few people, she got into the swing of things, posing for photos with various costumed people and handing over her phone so that someone else could snap the pictures. Her kids would surely be tickled by photos of old Mom with Batman and Robin.

After an hour or so, Olive realized she'd skipped breakfast and then walked out on lunch, so all she'd had that day was a cup of coffee followed by a few sips of wine. Her stomach was churning like an angry sea.

The concession area was filled with—of course—more costumed characters in various positions of repose, eating hotdogs, drinking sodas, and laughing as they talked and showed one another pictures on their phones. Olive got in line at a food stand and ordered a cheeseburger and onion rings with a Diet Coke.

Tray in hand, she wandered around looking for an empty seat at one of the tables, but had almost given up when she saw a hand in the air waving her over. It was the guy from her travel group who always seemed to be wearing some sort of superhero garb. Eddie, or Edward, she thought.

"Hi! Edgar," he said, holding out a hand and standing as Olive drew closer. "You look like you could use a friend to sit with."

Edgar. There it was. "I'm Olive," she said, setting her tray on the table and pulling out the chair. "And thank you for the invite. I came here on a whim today and realized after meeting Spiderman, Batman, a bunch of girls in patent leather shorts, and The Joker, that I hadn't bothered to eat yet. I'm famished." In one swift movement, she dropped her purse onto her lap and picked up her cheeseburger, taking an enormous bite. "Mmm," Olive said, nodding at the burger in her hand. "Vish ish goot."

Edgar laughed. "I love a woman with an appetite. And one who keeps the conversation flowing even while she's eating."

Olive put a hand over her mouth and blushed; she normally had far better table manners than that. "Sorry," she said, swallowing and washing the bite down with a big swig of Diet Coke. "I didn't mean to do that."

"Hey," Edgar said, raising both hands. "You're amongst friends. Chow down, girl."

Olive laughed. "I kind of feel like a kid being here," she admitted, taking a smaller bite of her burger and reaching for an onion ring. "I was supposed to be out doing grown-up stuff today, but I had a change of plans and decided to just walk in."

"Well that's got to be one of the best choices you've ever made," Edgar said with a smile. "Excepting, of course, the day you married your husband," he nodded at her wedding ring, "and the births of your children, assuming you've been blessed with them."

Olive glanced at her ring finger and then smiled at Edgar, who, though clearly quirky, was obviously a very sweet man. "Yes, you're right," she said, nodding. "Hanging out with superheroes in Edinburgh is a close second to the births of my four children."

Edgar laughed and slapped the table. "There we go! Now, where is the husband today? Forgive me for prying, but I did see you two together this morning in the lobby of the hotel, correct?"

"You did," Olive said, munching an onion ring. She was starting to feel infinitely better now that the food was hitting her bloodstream. "Dane and I decided to do separate things today after attending Easter services," she said, waving off the idea of spending time with her husband on a vacation that they were clearly taking together.

Edgar watched her as she ate. He'd finished his own lunch and was sitting with an empty tray in front of him, hands folded on his lap. "I was never so lucky myself," he said, looking off into the distance. "I met a lady once and thought I might like to wake up to her everyday for the rest of my life, but as it turned out, life had other things in store for us." He smiled wistfully and Olive stopped chewing.

"I'm so sorry," she said, for lack of anything better.

"Oh, don't be. I think the people we're meant to spend our lives with find their way to us, and the people who are not meant for us fall by the wayside. It's just how life works. As for children, I wouldn't have minded a few of those myself, but that didn't really happen either."

Olive sipped her Diet Coke through the straw as she looked at Edgar's face. "It's not too late. You're a man—you've got forever, right?"

Edgar chuckled and folded his arms across his chest. "I don't know about forever," he said, "but I guess technically I still have some time. Maybe I'll meet a nice Scottish lass and make a go of it, huh?"

Olive smiled at him, grateful to be lunching with someone whose sense of humor seemed steady and easy. "Hey," she said, crumpling up the wrapper to her burger and starting in on the rest of her onion rings. "As this is my first time going to a comic book convention, do you think I could possibly tag along with you for a bit? I mean, only if it's not a problem. I won't slow you down though—I walk fast."

Edgar laughed again. "Young lady, you may join me for as long as you wish, and I will not require you to walk fast. We'll just mosey along and see what there is to see."

"I do love being called 'young lady,'" Olive said, dipping her onion ring into the sauce that had come with them, "but I'm afraid I'm not that young."

Edgar frowned. "Was Regan in office at any point during your childhood?"

"Yes."

"Did you come straight home from school and tune in to MTV hoping to catch Michael Jackson's 'Thriller'?"

Olive nodded.

"I see. And by any chance did you or anyone you knew as a teenager drive a Pinto?"

Olive choked on her soda and nodded, patting her chest as she did. "Yes," she wheezed. "My first boyfriend drove a Pinto!"

"Then you, my friend, are only as old as you feel. You and I are about the same age, and I have news for you: we're just getting start-ed." Edgar stood up and tossed their used napkins onto his empty tray. "I'll just throw this away and then whenever you're ready, we'll head out in search of our next superhero of the day."

* * *

When Olive and Edgar burst through the doors of the hotel and into the lobby, she found Dane waiting there, sitting in a chair at a table by the window. He looked lost, forlorn, apologetic. And then his eyes landed on Edgar, standing there next to Olive and smiling like a man who'd just had a fabulous date, and he started to look angry.

"Olive," Dane said in a demanding tone. "What the hell is going on? Where were you? I tried calling and you didn't even—"

Olive held up a hand to stop him. "I'm fine. I went to the Comic Con and ran into Edgar, who is part of our tour group. Edgar, this is my husband Dane." Olive started to introduce the men to each other, but Dane jumped up and walked the few steps between his chair and where Olive and Edgar stood. Without hesitation, he grabbed his wife by the elbow—not roughly, but proprietarily—and steered her toward the hallway without a word to Edgar or a handshake or even an acknowledgment.

"Olive," Edgar called, "I'll hang onto your t-shirt and the other stuff you bought."

Dane's grip tightened on Olive's arm and they kept walking.

"Dane," Olive said in a strained voice, "let me go."

"Let you go? You took off at lunch, left me sitting there like a fool at Maison Bleue, and now you show up *hours* later with some guy, having had the time of your life at a what? A comic book show?"

Olive wrested her arm free. "It was a Comic Con—where superheroes meet with fans and you can take pictures and dress up if you want."

Dane took the key card from his jacket pocket and swiped it to open the door to their first floor room. He didn't push her into the room, but the hand on her lower back strongly suggested that she enter. The door shut firmly behind them.

58

"I have no idea what's gotten into you," Dane said, sitting on the edge of the bed and putting a hand to his forehead. "Do you know how much of an ass I look like with my wife running around Edinburgh, not taking my calls? Do you? What would your children say if they knew you ditched their father mid-lunch to go on a date with some extremely weird-looking guy—"

"Dane." Olive cut him off. "I was not on a date. And please don't be unkind to Edgar. He's a nice man and I happened to run into him inside the convention while I was looking for a place to eat my lunch."

"You *had* a place to eat your lunch," Dane said with venom. He got to his feet. "And you walked out without provocation and just left. I don't even know who you are sometimes."

"You don't know who I am?" She looked at him with an incredulous frown. "Then how do you think I feel? You aren't even the same man I married." Her words got quiet as her heartbeat slowed in her chest. "People change over the years, Dane, but you..." She waved a hand over him, looking him up and down. "You look like my Dane, but you're not. You're some angry, possessive, unhinged version of the Dane I fell in love with."

As she spoke, Dane started to deflate. His face fell, and his shoulders hunched. "Olive, come on."

"No, you come on, Dane." Olive walked over to the dresser and yanked open a drawer. She pulled her clothes out and tossed them on the bed, walking around the room and gathering her other items. From the closet she dragged her suitcase.

"What are you doing?" Dane sounded bewildered.

Without pausing, Olive said: "I'm going to try to book a flight home for myself. And if I can't get one, then I'll get a different room."

"There's a comic book convention and a science convention happening in this city at the same time, Ol. You're not getting another room," Dane said. He sounded as if he'd be thrilled when she proved him right.

"Then I'll go straight to the airport and camp out there," Olive said petulantly, shoving her clothes and toiletries into the suitcase willy-nilly and zipping it shut. "I don't care. I'm just done with all this, Dane. DONE."

Dane stood in the middle of the room with his hands on his hips. Behind him, the plaid curtains were open to reveal a view of a side street, and the bed was neatly made up by housekeeping, pillows fluffed and straight, duvet pulled smooth. To Olive, he looked like a little boy who was in trouble but didn't know what to say.

Olive set her suitcase on its wheels and pulled out the handle. "I'm at a loss here, Dane." She pursed her lips and looked at him. "I guess I'll see you at home."

It felt ridiculous wheeling her luggage down the hall with no idea where she was going or what would happen next, but it also felt freeing in a way. As her footsteps fell quietly on the thick carpet, Olive held her head high. It was absolutely time for her to start setting some personal boundaries and accepting that she'd done everything she could to help her husband, but to little or no avail.

"Olive!" A door to one of the rooms opened and Lucy stepped out. She was grinning at Olive, but the smile faded as she spotted the suitcase and the set look on Olive's face. "What's going on? Is something wrong with your room?" Lucy stepped out into the hall, letting the door to her room close behind her.

"No," Olive said, standing there with the handle of her suitcase in one hand, her purse slung over her other shoulder. "There's something wrong with my marriage."

"Been there," Lucy said, not missing a beat. She glanced up and down the hall. "How about you come in for a few minutes? Rather than us standing here and talking about personal stuff in the hall."

Olive looked toward the lobby. The front desk was in sight, and she knew that if she made it there she could beg for an empty broom closet to sleep in, or ask them to call an Uber to the airport. Either way, she'd be taking an important step in the direction of reclaiming herself. She looked at Lucy's gentle smile and decided to go in and talk to her for a few minutes.

"Here," Lucy said, taking the handle of Olive's suitcase and leaving it by the door as she pointed at the small bistro table with two chairs by the window. Rather than a view of a charming side street with foot traffic, Lucy's window looked out on a tiny garden that was fenced in by short wooden pickets. It teemed with wet, luscious flowers, dripping with the light rain that seemed to steadily fall, but bursting with color. "Sit," Lucy said, directing a still-stunned Olive to a chair, which she took.

"I'm sorry to stop you from wherever you were going," Olive said, remembering her manners as she sat in the middle of Lucy's room. Rather than one king-sized bed, she had two smaller ones, but other than that, the plaid curtains were the same, as were the green corduroy duvets and the side tables.

"You're not stopping me from anything." Lucy sat in the chair opposite hers. "Now what happened, if you don't mind my asking."

Olive heaved a huge, soul-weary sigh and set her elbows on the table. "We went to church," she started, remembering that it was still Easter. "And it was lovely. Then Dane had booked a reservation for lunch at an amazing restaurant, which shocked me. Things were going well until...actually," she frowned, squinting at a spot high on the wall. "I'm not sure what went wrong. He was talking about therapy, and I suddenly realized that I've put all this time into making him feel like himself again, while at the same time I was having little crises of my own that I had to push under the rug. I think we all question who we are and where we're going at this point of our lives, but I haven't had that luxury."

Lucy nodded, chewing on her lower lip as she listened. She folded her arms across her chest and leaned back in her chair, watching Olive's expressive face.

"I know this all sounds like a whole heap of first world problems," Olive said, looking embarrassed. "You know, 'Oh, poor me. No one wants to listen to *my* problems.' But it's not just that," she said slowly, thinking as she spoke. "It's more that I can't even put myself first when I need to. I tell myself to just shut up and ignore the nagging feelings, and to focus on Dane because his needs are bigger."

"And do you really think they are?"

Olive shrugged. "I'm not sure anymore. I told you the whole story about Catherine and all the things that rained down on him, but can't we move past that at some point? Can't he just accept that life isn't always the way you think it's going to be, and that people are going to let you down sometimes? Why does it always have to come back to how betrayed *he* feels?"

Lucy kept her eyes on Olive's face. She knew that all these questions were rhetorical, and that her job was to simply be there. To be present for Olive, who it seemed had had no one to listen to her in these past few years.

Olive took a deep breath and straightened her spine. "I'm really sorry to have dumped all of this on you during your trip, Lucy. You didn't ask for this when a strange couple from San Diego signed up to join you in Edinburgh."

"Stop. Don't even give it a second thought," Lucy assured her, reaching across the table to touch her hand. "When I left my old career, I wasn't even sure that I'd be good at dealing with people who were still alive. I didn't know how to look at them and their lives and figure out what they needed. I'd gotten so good at looking at people who were no longer with us, and it was easy for me to assess them in parts or to guess how they'd gotten to where they were."

"You mean laying on a cold table in front of you?"

"Exactly," Lucy said. "But it's much more challenging for me to, say, look at you and imagine all the things that have gotten you to where you are. And I'm finding that I really do like that particular challenge."

"Well, given the fact that you went to med school, it probably wouldn't take you too long to shift gears and go into therapy. You're patient and a good listener, so maybe you were just in the wrong part of the medical field."

Lucy smiled. "Nah. I loved it—don't get me wrong. I never felt I was in the wrong area, I just needed a change. Sometimes that's what we all need."

Olive's eyes welled with tears and she nodded.

"So, to that end, why don't we solve problem number one here and give you a small change of scenery." Lucy patted Olive's hand and then sat back in her chair. "There are no rooms anywhere around here, which I know because I was warned about that when I booked this trip months ago. And flying home seems like a huge move on Easter when all that happened—and believe me, I'm not minimizing it—is that you and Dane had a disagreement over lunch."

Olive looked at the table sheepishly; when Lucy put it like that, it did sound idiotic.

"How about you crash with me for one night? I promise I don't snore." She smiled at Olive. "And then you can look at everything with fresh eyes tomorrow and decide how you feel. What do you think?"

Olive looked around. "Are you sure you wouldn't mind having a stranger in your space? It's a very generous offer, but I don't want to be that tour group guest who you talk about on the next trip."

Lucy laughed. "You think I'm going to tell stories about you to everyone who joins me in Morocco for May Day?"

A smile spread across Olive's face. "I wouldn't blame you: Crazy Woman Flees Own Husband and Crashes Tour Group Leader's Hotel Room. Cleans Out Mini-bar and Trashes Room," Olive said, making it sound like a headline in a newspaper.

"Hey," Lucy said, still laughing. "I can do you one better and tell you a story about our trip to St. Barts last month, but only if you promise not to tell a single soul."

Olive grew serious and held up a hand. "Scout's honor."

"Okay," Lucy moved around in her chair and sat up tall like she was about to divulge a very important state secret. "Here's the dirt: a certain tour group leader whose name shall not be mentioned drank *far too much* on a yacht one evening—totally uncharacteristic of her, I might add—and woke up the next morning married to a stranger."

Olive's mouth dropped open and she made a shocked sound. "Lucy!"

"Yep. And it gets better: the stranger was a member of my tour group. And ten years younger than me."

"LUCY!" Olive yelped, putting a hand in front of her mouth. "I need more details."

"Well," Lucy shrugged, looking pleased with how much she'd shocked poor Olive. "I guess you're going to have to bunk with me for a night then, because those are the kind of details I only share during a sleepover with candy and face masks."

Olive couldn't stop the laughter from bubbling out of her. "Okay, you got it," she said. "It's a deal. And thank you, Lucy." Olive looked at her searchingly. "I really appreciate it."

"Girl," Lucy said, winking at Olive. "Don't you even sweat it for one second. I just want to keep my eye on you so that you don't wander this city alone and wake up married to some hot Scot."

Chapter 9

April 16
Edinburgh

Lucy woke up early to give Olive some time to herself, dressing quietly and packing a day bag to take with her as she hit the streets of Edinburgh. It was a free day for everyone to come and go as they pleased, or to just hang out at the hotel if they so chose. Lucy was finding on these trips that having a little unplanned time was always a good thing for the travelers, not to mention for herself.

With a biscuit in one hand and coffee in a paper to-go cup in the other, Lucy walked out of the hotel and set off in the direction of the building that housed the Edinburgh Science Festival. She felt a spring in her step after finally acclimating to the time zone, and she'd slept like a rock the night before, even while sharing her room with Olive.

For her part, Olive had talked a bit while she lay under the covers in her matching flannel pajama top and bottoms, laughing as Lucy recounted in more detail her fake and accidental wedding to Finn Barlow on the trip to St. Barts. Olive had talked about her adult children and how proud they made her, and she'd listened as Lucy talked a bit about her mother and her old life in Buffalo, then they'd turned off their lamps and fallen asleep before eleven.

The Edinburgh Science Festival had piqued the interest of a few of the guests, but none so much as Lucy, who had a particular interest (still, and probably forever) in anything to do with forensics. She was also looking forward to a lecture called "The Secrets of Healthy Cognitive Aging" that she hoped would give her some insight into her mother's declining mental state, and honestly, to just being on her own for the day.

By the time she'd checked in and presented the ticket she'd purchased online, Lucy had finished her biscuit and coffee and was ready to explore. This was a rare treat: indulging in her passion for science and medicine while still technically doing her new job. So far it had seemed like, in order to be successful, she needed to completely devote herself to travel and advertising the trips and so she had, but to check out for a few hours and just take in the science exhibits felt like a little slice of heaven to her.

In the midst of wandering through a display of the world's most bizarre things ever discovered on x-rays (a lightbulb lodged in a small intestine; a nail wedged into the roof of a person's mouth and running straight into their brain), Lucy's watched buzzed. Nick was calling.

"Hi," she answered, a smile on her face. "What are you doing awake?"

"It's six o'clock and Hemingway wanted me to get up and let him out," he said, sounding a little groggy. "How are things in the 'Land of the Brave'?"

Lucy sighed and stepped away from the x-ray displays so that she could find a spot to talk. She chose a bench situated in an all-black hallway with a direct view of a skeleton under a spotlight. The effect would have been spooky to the uninitiated, but something about it comforted her.

"I shared my room last night," she said cryptically, half-teasing him and expecting him to pick up on her reference to the crazy-drunken-sham-wedding in St. Barts.

Nick went silent. "What?" he said, sounding perplexed and hurt.

"Oh, god! Nick! No, not like that," Lucy said hurriedly, realizing too late that they didn't yet have their own shorthand for teasing. "I was just trying to make it sound wild. Never mind." She shook her head and waved a hand like she could erase the bad joke. "The real story is that I have a married couple on my trip. They're in their fifties and going through a real shake-up of some sort. It's a long story, but I caught the wife with her suitcase packed yesterday, ready to head to the airport. I invited her in and she ended up sleeping in my spare bed so they could both cool off. That's all."

Nick stayed quiet for a second. "Well, I guess that's better than waking up next to some guy," he said, aiming for casual humor but falling short. "Anyway, that's crazy. Things okay with them today?"

"I'm not sure, to be honest. I wanted to come to the Edinburgh Science Festival, so I left Olive in my room and headed over here. I've got a full day of super-nerdy things to see and do, and I'm honestly looking forward to being alone." She looked at the way the spotlight shining on the lone skeleton cast a glossy glow on the black floor around it. "I do wish you were here, though. You're the one person I wouldn't mind spending the day with."

Nick laughed roughly, sounding very much like a man who was still horizontal and shrouded in nothing but bedsheets and a smile. "Oh yeah?"

"Yeah," Lucy said, suddenly feeling shy. She'd been busy so far in Edinburgh, and missing Nick had been pushed to the back burner. "I loved having you on St. Barts with me."

"If I hadn't come along, maybe we wouldn't have..."

"Yeah, we might not have," Lucy finished his thought. "But I'm glad we did."

They were both silent for a moment, letting that thought sit there in the middle of the miles that separated them.

"How long till you come home? I'm not asking for me, just so you know," Nick clarified. "It's actually for Hemmie. He thinks you're cute."

"Oh?" Lucy laughed. "Well, tell him I'll be there in four days, okay?"

"Four whole days..." Nick sounded like he was rolling over in bed. "Yeah, I guess he can make it that long. I'll distract him with walks on the beach and extra treats."

"What about you?" Lucy hedged. "Do you miss me?"

"Of course I do. I unlock the door to The Carrier Pigeon every morning and it takes me a few minutes to remember that I won't see you walking past my windows on your way to the office."

"Awww. I miss you too, you know."

Nick made a sound like he was about to say something but then stopped and cleared his throat instead.

"You okay?" Lucy asked.

"Yeah," Nick said, sounding decidedly not okay. "It's just...this is dumb."

"Tell me."

"I just wanted to warn you that I know I sound like a high schooler here. But I went into Beans & Sand yesterday, and Dev made this big deal about how he'd heard from you and how you guys had been talking business stuff for months about your trips. And he brought up the concert again."

Lucy made a face to herself and clenched her fist, which she pounded against her knee. Weren't they all perpetually high schoolers when it came to stuff like this? She knew that navigating matters of the heart wasn't something that you automatically mastered at some particular age, so it didn't bother her that Nick was feeling this one out. What bothered her was that Dev was somehow giving Nick the impression that Lucy was flirting with him or reaching out to him in a romantic way.

"Dev has definitely been my sounding board about the trips," Lucy said, still pounding her thigh lightly with her fist as she spoke. "He's had some good ideas. As for the concert, it was fun. I guess you could call it a date, though nothing date-like happened."

"Lucy, you don't have to—" Nick sounded chagrined at making her explain the concert, but Lucy cut him off.

"No, it's fine," she said. "I like Dev. He's an interesting character, and he really has given me some good ideas for advertising my business. But I definitely don't like him the way I like you." *Okay*, she thought. *That felt a little high school.* But Lucy forged ahead. "I don't want you to ever think there's something going on there when there isn't. I've had my heart played with more than once, and I wouldn't do that to you, Nick."

He was quiet, and she could picture him sitting up in bed, rubbing his unshaven face as Hemingway jumped up onto the bed and sat next to him.

"Got it?" Lucy said, prodding him.

"Got it."

"Now, I have a lecture to attend about cognitive impairment, and I still need to see the exhibit on death and decomposition in forensic science."

"Okay, gross." Nick laughed. "I know people are usually either inclined toward science and math, or they lean more toward creative things, and it's clear that you and I exemplify that. I'd rather gouge my eyes out than spend a day thinking about science. Now if there were a literature convention, I could get lost in that."

"And for me, nothing would put me to sleep faster than a lecture on Shakespeare or Dante."

"Dante?" Nick sounded surprised. "Someone took a lit class or two in college."

"Had to. But don't get me wrong—I love to read. I just wouldn't roll up my sleeves and spend a day discussing dead authors."

"I hear you."

"Anyway, I should probably get to the lecture I want to attend and then finish working my way through this place. I've got a dinner planned with my travel group tonight, though to be perfectly honest, what I really want is to click my heels three times and be at home."

"You're not having fun?" Nick sounded worried.

"No, no—I am. I just hit this point in a trip, as most people do, when I long for my own bed and the familiar trappings of home."

"Understood. Now, get out there and look at some decaying bodies or whatever, then head to dinner with these people. Next time we talk I want to hear more about the superhero guy you texted me about."

"Deal." Lucy smiled to herself and wished for a moment that they were FaceTiming so that she could see Nick and Hemingway waking up and getting their day started. "Talk to you soon, yeah?"

"I'm right here."

"And I'm right here. Miss you—bye." Lucy waited a beat.

"Bye."

With a sigh, she stood up and put her phone into her purse, zipped it, and walked directly toward the skeleton she'd been staring at the whole time.

It took mere seconds for her to be totally engrossed in the various intricacies of what different cancers did to the human body, how pond water decayed human organs, and the lecture on cognitive decline. When Lucy finally left the building several hours later, it was with a head full of the things she'd spent so much of her working life studying and dealing with, and a heart that was ready to tackle the rest of the trip.

The Plaid Duck was set for their party of twenty-eight that evening, and Lucy arrived with the entire Holiday Adventure Club group after a brisk walk through the evening drizzle. She took off her coat and a concierge greeted them all at the door, pointing them to racks so that they could let their umbrellas and jackets drip-dry while they ate.

A room in the back of the restaurant had been set for the large group, and on a buffet table were various small plates: charcuterie boards spread with cured meats, olives, bread, oatcakes, and apple chutney; a selection of Scottish cheeses; polenta and parmesan donuts with whipped feta dip; fried anchovies; spiced lamb terrine with whipped mint crème fraîche; and little bites of haddock croquette with saffron mayo. A crackling fireplace was manned by an apron-wearing server who smiled at them as they entered, and a small bar was set in the corner so that the bartender's back was to the rain-covered window, his various bottles shining from the firelight and the dim lamps spread around the cozy private dining room.

"This looks amazing," Edgar said, putting his hands together as if in prayer and reaching for a small plate to fill with hors d'oeuvres. "I have no idea where to start."

"Start at the beginning and enjoy," Lucy said, patting him on the arm lightly as she moved over to where Vanderbilt, Snow, and Filene were huddled near the bar, figuring out what to order and looking every inch like eighteen-year-old American girls who still didn't have the legal right to drink in their own country.

"Ladies," Lucy said, stepping up to the bar but looking at the three girls. "How are things? I feel like I haven't seen much of you."

"Snow met a guy and he had some friends, so we've been hanging out with them," Filene said, tossing her hair over one shoulder and looking around at the rest of the group as they mingled, chose seats at the tables spread around the room, and filled plates from the buffet. "Not that it isn't fun to hang out with a bunch of grandparents, but..." Filene's eyes skipped over people who were clearly at least three times her age.

Lucy smiled at them patiently. "Did you manage to get to the Comic Con and check things out?"

"We went in. Lots of nerds," Snow said.

"So I guess the answer to 'Did you hit the Science Convention' is also going to be a no," Lucy said.

"Oh my god," Vanderbilt snorted. "Yeah. Hard no on that one."

"So who is this guy you met?" Lucy tried to make the question sound more like curious girl-talk and less like a snoopy mom sticking her nose into her kid's business.

"Drake," Snow said. "He's part of a motorcycle gang."

"Um," Lucy said, immediately on high alert. "What?"

"No he's not," Filene said firmly, smacking Snow's arm with the back of her hand. "He just *rides* a motorcycle. It's not like that."

"Filene," Snow said with urgency in her voice. "Haven't you seen *Sons of Anarchy*? Drake and Will and Benny are definitely in a gang."

"They're not, and we're fine," Filene said to Lucy, giving her a tight smile. She grabbed Snow by the arm and steered her and Vanderbilt toward the appetizers. As they moved away, walking closely like they were somehow attached to one another, Lucy could hear snippets of their hissed conversation.

None of this was good news, and she was still frowning over the information about Drake, Will, Benny, and their motorcycle gang when Edgar appeared at the bar next to her.

"Get you a drink, milady?" Edgar offered, nodding at the bar. "I took the liberty of saving you a seat at my table, but will not be offended in the slightest if you'd prefer to mingle."

"No, that would be wonderful. Thank you." Lucy smiled at him, but felt distracted. "And I'd love a glass of red wine, if you don't mind."

"Then it shall be yours," Edgar said with a small bow. "Our table is over there by the fireplace."

"Thanks, Edgar. I'm going to get a few appetizers." Lucy walked away from him, the events of the day spinning through her mind: her conversation with Nick that had hedged into teenage territory with talk of Dev; the lecture she'd attended where the neurologist speaking had given the grim realities of living with someone who has dementia; the thought of three young girls in her group running around with a Scottish biker gang.

She hadn't lied to Nick earlier when she said that she wished she could be at home, and as she picked up a warm plate and filled it with bite-size delicacies, a deep well of homesickness opened up inside of her. The rain streamed down the windows all around the private dining room, and the dark night outside looked lonely and uninviting. Maybe she could just stay in this room all night and avoid the cold walk back to the hotel. And perhaps if she sat by the fire and sipped a glass of wine, she'd feel reinvigorated and ready to push through the last few days in Edinburgh.

"You look chilly," Olive said, smiling at Lucy as she walked over to her with a plate in one hand and a glass of wine in the other. "Maybe you should move closer to the fire."

"My thoughts exactly," Lucy agreed, nodding at the table that Edgar had saved for them. "In fact, I was heading to that one right there. Want to join?"

Olive's head swiveled and she scanned the room for Dane, who was standing near the buffet table, deep in conversation with another man who wore a strikingly similar outfit: khakis, brown lace-up shoes, and a navy blue sweater.

"Did Dane's twin brother join us?" Lucy teased.

Olive made a face. "Men of a certain age certainly fall into a very particular pattern of dressing, don't they? Same haircut, same stance," she said, observing the men as they spoke. And she wasn't wrong: Dane was stooped forward while he listened to the other, slightly shorter man, their faces etched with matching serious looks.

"How are things going today?" Lucy asked hesitantly. She'd gone back to the hotel in the late afternoon to change for dinner and found all of Olive's stuff gone from her room.

Olive paused as she formulated a response. "Things are okay. I agreed to stay for the rest of the trip, but we're at a bit of a stalemate." She put a hand to her forehead and rubbed it gently. "I'm not sure where to go next. But I am really grateful to you for last night." Olive let her hand fall from her forehead as she met Lucy's eye. "I would have left in a fit and then probably regretted it, and I also really enjoyed just chatting with you and having a girls' night."

"Hey, I enjoyed it too," Lucy said. "Let's sit."

They got settled at the table by the fireplace and glanced at the menu as they nibbled appetizers, exchanging pleasantries with Edgar and debating the potential merits of the steak with wild garlic and pumpkin seed dressing versus the slow roasted pork belly with mint yogurt as a main dish. Dane was on his way to their table with a full plate and a glass of bourbon as Lucy bit into one of the savory donuts dipped in whipped feta.

"Oooh, this is *amazing*," Lucy said, covering her mouth with one hand closing her eyes as she chewed. "I hadn't realized how hungry I was. Maybe all I needed was some food."

Dane pulled out the fourth chair and Edgar pushed back his own, standing to shake Dane's hand and introduce himself, as they hadn't properly met yet, given Dane's frosty attitude following the Comic Con.

"I'm Edgar—" he started to say, holding out his hand. But his words were drowned out by the loud roar of motorcycles, their headlights visible outside the restaurant windows as a long line of bikes came to a stop on the rain-slicked streets just beyond the glass. Every head in the private room turned to look at where the noise was coming from, but Lucy's eyes went immediately to the only people in the room who looked giddy rather than surprised: Filene, Vanderbilt, and Snow.

Lucy stood immediately and strode over to where they were standing, ready to tell them that their friends were not invited to the private dinner that was taking place. But before she could, Snow rushed to the window with palpable excitement and put both hands to the glass like a girl watching Santa's reindeer and sleigh landing on her front lawn.

"We're out of here," Vanderbilt said, reaching for Filene. "Let's roll. Snow, pull it together," she said, clapping her hands to break the spell that appeared to have been cast over the wide-eyed girl at the window.

Within seconds, the trio had grabbed their purses, abandoned the cocktails they'd finally gotten up the nerve to order, and were racing for the door.

"Ladies," Lucy called, feeling her heart leap into her throat as her eyes cut to the men standing on the street, their figures lit up by the old-fashioned street lamps that caught black leather and rain-drops in their glow. "I don't think this is a good idea," she said loudly, knowing that there was no way she'd be heard over the still-revving motorcycle engines. "Filene!" she shouted as a last resort, hoping to appeal to the girl who appeared to have the most common sense of the three.

But the door was already swinging shut behind Filene as Lucy's words crossed her lips, and with that, they were gone.

* * *

Lucy had had to accept that it was the girls' right, as young adults, to leave the dinner, but it had troubled her as she'd watched helplessly through the window while they hiked up their skirts and climbed onto the back of the bikes of some extremely rough looking men.

Now, back at the hotel and sitting with Edgar and Olive on the stone step in front of the fireplace in the lobby, a fire roaring at their backs, Lucy waited while Dane paced back and forth, phone pressed to his ear as he listened to the advice of a friend he'd called to inquire about Lucy's rights and obligations to call the girls' parents.

"Yes," Dane said, nodding as he walked past them for what seemed like the millionth time. "They're all three eighteen. Mmhmm. I believe so." He put one hand over the receiver and stopped walking, turning to Lucy. "They all live with their parents?"

Lucy turned both palms to the ceiling. "Yes. They're about to graduate from high school."

Olive reached over and took Lucy's hand in hers. "Everything is going to be fine, Lucy," she promised. "I've raised four teenagers and they absolutely make terrible decisions sometimes, but these girls seem like good kids. I really think they'll be back soon."

"God, I hope so," Lucy said, squeezing Olive's hand.

Edgar cleared his throat. "You know," he started, putting his index finger to his lips and touching the end of his oversized nose with the tip of his finger. But instead of going on, he simply shook his head and squinted.

Both Lucy and Olive leaned forward on the stone step and looked at him, waiting for more. But before Edgar could speak, Dane hung up the phone and stood before them.

"So," Dane said, putting his phone into the back pocket of his pants. "That was my former coworker, Marcia Keller, and she's currently working for a law firm that specializes in international crime, human trafficking, and young adult offenders."

"But the girls aren't offenders," Lucy said quickly, nearly jumping to her feet. "They're the victims here."

Dane lowered his chin. "Lucy," he said, "they're young, yes, but unless these men have kidnapped them and are holding them against their will, they aren't necessarily victims. Unless they went with these guys willingly and then somehow ended up getting assaulted—"

"Oh!" Lucy said, standing up this time and letting go of Olive's hand. "Please don't say that. I've done far too many postmortem examinations on women who were assaulted, and to even think for one second that these girls, no matter how sassy and naïve they are, might be mistreated by a bunch of grown men..." Lucy put both hands over her face and took a deep breath. One in, one out. Another in, another out. Finally, having calmed herself just a little, she pulled her hands away from her face and straightened her shoulders. Her back was hot from sitting so close to the fire, but her hands felt ice cold from the fear.

Dane held up a hand. "Let's not go too far down that path, okay? Marcia's advice was for you to call their parents. She said that even as legal adults in their home country, they're still on a trip with your group under the express understanding by their parents that there's *some* sort of supervision or safety provided by the travel group. To not call them would be remiss—possibly legally—but as a parent, I can say it would be morally remiss. I would absolutely want to know if either of my daughters had been in this situation as eighteen year olds."

"Or our sons," Olive added, looking at Dane sternly.

"Of course," he agreed, nodding at her. "I wasn't trying to be sexist, but we're all adults here. We know the potential for danger that could befall three unworldly teenage girls."

The four of them went silent, all lost in their own thoughts about the situation. As much as Lucy knew she should be thinking of covering her own ass here as the owner of the travel agency, her real concern was for the safety of the girls. She'd not only been an unworldly teenage girl at one point, but she was a grown woman who'd seen too much tragedy firsthand. She'd never sleep that night if she didn't keep moving ahead to get Snow, Vanderbilt, and Filene back to the hotel safely.

"Okay," she said, making a decision. "I'm going to go to my room and get on my computer to access all three girls' emergency contact information. I'll call their parents and calmly let them know that they've gone out with a group of men." She paused here, closing her eyes for a second. "God, this all sounds terrible, doesn't it? 'Hi, I'm calling to let you know I've lost your daughters—just temporarily though! Yes, they disappeared on the motorcycles of some grizzly older men. But I've got this under control.'"

"Well, when you put it that way, it sounds kind of atrocious," Olive said. She screwed up her face and thought for a second. "How about telling them that you felt obligated to let them know their daughters have taken up the company of some men who are known to be part of a biker gang but that—"

"Nope," Dane interrupted, shaking his head. "My heart would explode if I was the dad getting that phone call."

Edgar finally spoke. "How about this," he said, looking back and forth between Lucy and Dane and Olive. "Dane, you said you knew someone who works for Police Scotland, right?"

"I do," Dane said with a single nod.

"Why don't you try to get ahold of that contact and see what you can find out about supposed 'biker gangs' in the area? Who are they, where do they congregate, who are the known members?"

"I'll take notes," Olive said, stepping over to stand next to her husband. "We can get that information."

"Okay," Edgar turned to Lucy. "And how about if you postpone calling their parents for an hour or two. It's still just late afternoon in the States, and with that extra couple of hours, you and I can go back to the restaurant and see if there's anything we can find out from people in that area. We'll act like street cops and ask a few questions."

Lucy nodded, thinking about it. "I guess we could do that," she said. "We could get out there and see what the locals know."

"So that's what we'll do then," Dane said. "Olive and I will get ahold of my friend somehow and ask a few questions. Lucy, I trust you have our cell numbers?"

"I do," she said. "And Olive has mine, so you guys contact us if you find out anything, and we'll do the same."

Olive looked at her watch. "It's eight forty-five now, so let's touch bases at ten o'clock no matter what. Deal?"

"Got it." Lucy grabbed her purse from the stone step in front of the fireplace; the leather had warmed up and felt like a heating pad against her body as she strapped it across her chest. "Let's head out, Edgar."

"You got it, boss," he said, letting one hand hover politely near the middle of Lucy's back as she pushed through the door and out onto the street. "Let's get this fixed."

Chapter 10

April 16
Edinburgh

The house was dark and pulsing with music from a speaker that was covered in empty beer bottles and red plastic cups. Men in black leather with droopy eyes were splayed across couches and spilled into chairs all around the front room, and women in tight jeans and tiny shirts wound around the furniture to deliver newly opened bottles of beer and to perch on the laps of whoever pulled them close.

Snow stood near the entrance to the kitchen, her upper lip curled in distaste. This was nothing like the parties she'd gone to back home, and when Drake had mentioned a party with friends, she'd been envisioning something involving a keg, maybe a drunken card game, and most likely some whisky-flavored kisses. But as she looked around the room, scanning for Drake, her eyes landed on a girl in a minuscule plaid school girl skirt straddled across the lap of Will, who'd brought Vanderbilt on the back of his bike.

"Oh my god," Filene said, making a face almost identical to Snow's as she unscrewed the cap of a tube of lipgloss. "This place is filthy."

Vanderbilt leaned forward so that she could look at Filene from the other side of Snow, shooting her an accusatory look. "Were you imagining a swimming pool and a maid, Filene? We actually came here with a bunch of guys who have rancid b.o. and probably haven't showered in, like, days."

Filene's eyes widened; it hadn't occurred to her that humans went days without showering outside of a camping trip or maybe prison. "God..." she whispered. "Maybe we should get out of here."

Still leaning forward, Vanderbilt hissed at her: "How in the hell are we getting out of here? We're in the middle of nowhere, it's raining, and I'm guessing there isn't just an Uber around the corner."

It was true: they'd ridden down long, winding lanes on the back of the motorcycles, thrilling at the black night, the feel of cold, misty rain on their faces, and the way the headlights chased across the dark hills around them. But now that carefree joy had given way to reality, and none of the girls were nearly as impressed as they thought they'd be.

"Hey, lass," Drake said, appearing behind them from the kitchen and snaking an arm around Snow's waist. "You want to get a drink?"

Snow shook her head ever so slightly, hoping that he wouldn't take offense at her rejection of his offer. "No, I'm okay," she said weakly, offering him a tepid smile.

"You come to our place, you drink," Drake said definitively. Without waiting for an answer, he steered Snow across the room with him, leaving Filene and Vanderbilt to stare after them with open mouths.

It was then that Vanderbilt noticed Will with the oversized schoolgirl in his lap on the couch.

"Excuse me?" she said, putting one hand on her hip as she stared at the scene. "Who does this girl think she is?"

"Vandy," Filene said quietly, reaching out to tug on her friend's arm. "Let it go."

"No way," Vanderbilt said loudly, shooting poisonous darts at the back of the girl on Will's lap. Neither of them seemed to notice her ire, and what had just been a lap-sit turned into a long kiss right there in front of everyone. Vanderbilt yanked her arm free from Filene's grasp.

"Listen," Filene said, hoping that her friend would hear the voice of reason and be calmed. "You don't want that guy, Van. If we were at home you'd never look twice at him, unless it was to piss off your parents. Let it go."

Vanderbilt's shoulders dropped a few inches and Filene sensed that maybe she'd gotten through to her.

"I guess," Vanderbilt said.

"I'm right. And we need to get Snow," Filene added, trying to stay calm. Drake took her down a hallway, and I do not trust that guy."

It was as if a spell had been broken and Vanderbilt turned and looked Filene in the eye. "Oh, you don't trust him? You think? We're eighteen, Filene. We're here with a bunch of...of *men*. I'm pretty sure most of these guys have kids. Maybe some even have a motorcycle *and* a car."

"Yeah, maybe," Filene agreed mildly. "Now let's stick together. Hold my hand, okay?"

Vanderbilt laced her fingers through Filene's and held on tightly. "We need to find Snow."

Together, the girls picked their way through the front room, stepping over an enormous red-bearded biker who appeared to have passed out on the floor. Around him lay several empty alcohol bottles, but no one seemed concerned. Filene held Vanderbilt's hand tighter.

A fog of smoke hung in the air near the couches, and there was the distant smell of vomit and blood, though both girls walked with a hand over their noses, keeping their eyes trained on the hallway and knowing they'd find Snow in one of the rooms.

"There'll be a charge to pass," a short, red-eyed man in a leather vest with nothing beneath it said in a deep Scottish accent, wobbling on his feet as he leaned in to Vanderbilt with his lips puckered for a kiss. Everyone around him roared with laughter.

"Ew," Vanderbilt said, pulling away. "No. We're trying to find our friend."

"And find 'er you will," the man said, putting one hand against the nearest wall for support as he swayed on his feet. "Plus a whole heap o' trouble to boot!" Again, the laughter.

Filene pulled Vanderbilt along and they walked down the hall, ignoring the hoots that followed.

Hesitantly, Filene knocked on the first door and pushed it open ever so slightly. Although she herself wasn't a smoker, she definitely knew the smell of marijuana, and when she spotted two women in tank tops bent over what looked like a giant glass bong, she pulled the door shut again.

She was about to do the same thing at the next door—with Vanderbilt essentially glued to her side anxiously—when they heard a scream from down the hall followed by a man's loud, gruff admonishment and what sounded like a hard slap.

"Oh my god," Vanderbilt said, wrapping both hands around Filene's upper arm and holding it in a death grip.

"Yeah," Filene said, stepping away from the door she'd been about to open. "That's Snow."

* * *

"I wish you well on that one," a woman with crooked yellow teeth and eyes like a Basset Hound said, shaking her head. "Pity, that."

Edgar nodded and thanked her. His eyes cut to Lucy, who was standing next to him, face full of expectation.

"The Blue Angels," Edgar said, looking more than a little concerned. "Not just a bunch of punks on bikes."

"Are they bad?" Lucy knew less than nothing about biker gangs, though she'd seen her fair share of violence and destruction wrought by both gangs and motorcycles in her autopsy room over the years.

Edgar cleared his throat and swallowed at length. "Quite."

"Okay," Lucy said, nodding so quickly that it made her look like the kind of bobble-headed doll a person might put on their desk at work as a whimsical decoration. "Okay. Let's keep going." She looked at her watch: nine-forty.

They stood near the restaurant they'd eaten at earlier, The Plaid Duck, waiting to see if anyone worth talking to might pass by. As they did, two tough-looking young men approached on foot.

"Hello," Edgar called out, waving at them.

"Edgar," Lucy said quietly, hoping he wouldn't talk to them. Something about these guys looked menacing, and Lucy wanted to let them pass, but Edgar persisted.

"My friend and I are wondering if we could inquire just briefly about a group of men who seem to be causing us a bit of trouble."

"We'll cause you a bit more if you don't move out of our way, you tadger. And take the cow with you," the angry-looking one said, glancing at Lucy. The other guy gave a crooked smile of amusement.

"Fine sirs," Edgar went on, unwilling to be deterred from his mission. "Three young ladies who are traveling with our group have been, well, *abducted* is a strong word, but maybe 'absconded with' is better, by several men on motorcycles, and we're extremely concerned."

"As ya should be," the smirking man said, the smile falling from his face. "How young are the lasses?"

"Eighteen," Lucy confirmed, finding her voice and ignoring the fact that she'd been called a cow.

"Oooh," the first guy said, whacking his hand on the other guy's chest. "Ripe."

It took all the fortitude in Lucy's body not to lose it on these two. "They are extremely young and naïve, and they seem to have it in their heads that they've met some lovely young men while here in Edinburgh, but upon seeing these men, I can assure you that they are not the type of guys a mother would want to see her daughter vanish with."

"Are you the mother? You're quite a catch yourself," the mouthier guy said, openly looking Lucy up and down.

"No. For God's sake," Lucy said, trying not to roll her eyes and walk away. "I'm not their mother, but I am essentially in charge of their well-being. Now, do you know anything at all about a biker gang called the Blue Angels?"

The smirker sucked in air through his teeth and held up both hands. "Not a wise idea to mess with the Angels, lass," he said, shaking his head. "Count me out."

"We're not asking you to mess with them," Edgar said, stepping aside as a car whooshed past on the wet street, kicking up muddy rain water. They stood under a streetlamp that cast a yellow glow all around them. Lucy no longer felt afraid of these two men, just annoyed by their lack of concern and helpfulness. "What we need is any information you've got."

"Information, yeah?" the second guy said, lifting his chin a notch and narrowing his eyes. "You think you can give the Angels a run and grab three daft cows back from them? I dare you to try."

The first guy shrugged and pulled a pack of cigarettes from the breast pocket of his leather jacket. He appeared to have lost interest.

"Take a drive out to Leith," the second guy said, pointing out into the dark night. "You'll hear the sound of motorcycles and women screaming. If you hit the dock, you've gone too far."

And with that, they walked on, the glow of the first man's cigarette flaring as he turned his head to talk to his friend.

"Let's get a taxi," Edgar said, not wasting a second. "I think that's where we'll find them."

"Is that what your Spidey senses tell you?" Lucy wanted it to sound lighthearted, but she was too worried and instead it came out sounding a touch sarcastic.

But Edgar didn't seem to notice. "Indeed they do," he said, already pulling up the Uber app on his phone. "I'll get us a car, you send a message to Olive and Dane, alright?"

Lucy paused for a moment, admiring the earnest look on Edgar's face, and feeling a touch of softness toward this man she barely knew. His bald spot was the size of a small dinner plate, and a ring of salt and pepper hair circled his head like a halo. In the light of the street-lamp Lucy could see that his slightly old-fashioned eyeglasses were smudged. He was such a kind, good-hearted man, and she wished for him that he'd find someone to love him and all his quirks.

"You gonna message them, ya daft cow?" Edgar said, nudging her with an elbow and a smile so that she'd know he was teasing.

Lucy startled. "Yes. I'm on it."

She'd just opened a text to let Olive know that they were headed to a place called Leith with a dock to check things out when a silver Mercedes slid up to the curb and a man glanced their way from the dark interior, the dashboard lights lit up like an aircraft.

"Our chariot, milady," Edgar said, opening the back door for her. She climbed in and buckled her seatbelt, eyes turned to the windows of The Plaid Duck where servers in neat black aprons bustled around inside the cozy restaurant, clearing plates and smiling at patrons. If only she could turn back the hands of the clock a few hours and still be inside, sitting by the fire and enjoying a delicious meal instead of heading into the shadowy unknown. If only.

* * *

"What the hell is going on in here?" Filene demanded, pushing at the door from which she'd heard the scream just moments before. "Snow? Are you in there?" As she turned the knob, she realized it was locked and wouldn't give way. "Snow?" Filene pounded on the door first with a fist, then an open hand. "Open this damn door!" she shouted.

Next to her, Vanderbilt trembled, looking like a delicate flower caught in a rainstorm.

"Whoever is in there, open this door immediately," Filene demanded, sounding much fiercer than she felt. "Let me in or I'll break this door down. I swear to God I will!" She pounded the hollow wood with a fist again, turning her back on Vanderbilt as she did.

"Filene," Vanderbilt said, sounding shaky. "What if she's dead?"

"She's not dead," Filene hissed. "But she's definitely in trouble and we need to get in there."

Unbeknownst to the girls, just as Filene was about to pound the door with both fists in hopes of splintering the cheap wood and getting the attention of whoever was inside the room, Lucy and Edgar knocked on the front door. When no one answered, Edgar gave it one more hard rap and then opened it.

The scarred and weather-beaten door swung open to reveal a scene of debauchery that made Lucy and Edgar grimace: alcohol everywhere; women draped across men in various stages of undress; a cloud of smoke so heavy it looked like it was coming from a fog machine at a concert.

Lucy waved a hand in front of her face as she stepped in. "Well this is swanky," she said, taking a look around for any sign of the three girls. The music was loud and aggressive and other than a cursory glance, no one seemed bothered by Lucy and Edgar's entrance.

"They're in over their heads here," Edgar said, standing in the entryway with both hands on his hips. "None of this looks like the kind of mess I'd want to find my sister's kids in."

"This is not good," Lucy agreed. "I'll check the kitchen."

"I'm coming with you wherever you go in this house," Edgar said, staying close on her heels.

They made a quick scan of the galley kitchen and were confronted with a sink full of cigarette butts, empty cans, and food containers. In what would have been the dining room, someone had turned a table for eight over on its back, filled the hollow underside of the table with pillows and blankets, and now two naked women were tangled there, sleeping the sleep of the blackout drunk. The four legs of the table stood straight up in the air like bedposts, and Lucy stopped to observe the women for just a moment, tempted to roll them both onto their sides for fear they might vomit in their sleep.

"Not our concern right now," Edgar said as if he could read her mind. He grabbed her by the wrist to gently tug her along.

The hallway had four doors: one open to reveal a bathroom; two closed; and another ajar to reveal a young woman dancing slowly in front of four men, gyrating like a stripper without a pole. The curtains were shut tight and the room was lit only by a single red bulb. The woman dancing seemed totally lost in the moment, and after just a few seconds of watching, Lucy could see that Snow, Filene, and Vanderbilt were nowhere in sight.

Edgar was ready to knock on the first closed door when the one at the end of the hall swung open just enough to reveal the scene inside. Lucy turned to catch a glimpse of what—to her—looked like a war-torn hellscape.

Her heart nearly stopped.

Chapter 11

April 16

Edinburgh

After getting Lucy's message, Olive and Dane got their own Uber out to Leith with its dock and dark, wet streets. The driver pulled up to the address and, for just a brief moment, Dane hesitated, hand on the inside of the door as they sat in the warm, idling car and looked at the rundown house before them. The sound of the music inside pounded so hard that they could feel it even with the car doors closed.

"Ollie, this isn't even our business, really," Dane said, turning to look at his wife. "Don't you think it might be better to let Lucy handle this?"

Olive picked up her purse and threw open her car door. "No. I do not. I'm going in and if you want to just go on and Uber back to the hotel, then go for it." She closed the car door before Dane could respond, leaving him to either drive away like a coward, or get out and follow his wife like, well, a coward. He got out.

"Ollie," Dane called, walking fast to catch her on her way up to the front door. She was fearless, his wife, striding confidently into a situation she knew nothing about, all to help some dimwitted girls who didn't know enough not to get mixed up with a bunch of strange and dangerous men. He'd have throttled his own kids if they'd ever gotten caught in a pickle like this.

"Olive," he tried again, catching her on the front porch just before she knocked. "Let me go first. Please."

Olive stopped, hand poised to knock, and looked at her husband. He'd always been chivalrous, if nothing else, and she knew he'd never let her barge into a situation where she'd be in danger.

"I owe Lucy," Olive said, pulling the strap of her purse across her body firmly and running a hand through her windswept brown hair as it tickled her ears and chin. "She took me in and let me stay with her instead of rushing off to the airport and doing something I'd regret."

Dane looked down at her, watching the way the dim porch light caught on the diamond earrings he'd bought her for their twentieth anniversary. She'd deserved so much more than he'd given her over the years and he knew that now, but was it too late to turn things around.

"Ol," Dane said softly, his voice barely audible above the loud music coming from behind the door. "I've messed up a lot of things. I let life get the better of me for a long time and it took over. I don't know what else to say."

Olive nearly forgot about the mission they were on as she looked at her husband, waiting to hear what else he had to say. Her hand fell to her side and while she felt guarded, she was also curious.

"That night when Catherine—"

Olive held up a hand. "Please don't blame all this on your sister again."

"I'm not, Ol. I'm not," he said, reaching out and taking the hand she'd held up so that he could hold it in his. "It was just a huge shock. To find out that a simple genealogy test had unbraided the entire fabric of my family—I didn't even know who I was anymore." His eyes drifted toward the unkempt yard behind Olive. "Not to mention that I had no idea who my parents were."

"But you did, Dane. They were still the same people you'd always known."

He huffed. "Not even close. Can you imagine, Olive? Finding out that another man had fathered you and your siblings with your mom and she'd raised you like it had never happened?"

Olive took a beat before responding. They'd been down this road a time or two. "No, I can't really imagine it, but I also know in my heart that it wouldn't have made me love my parents any less. Life is complicated, Dane."

"Olive, my mother married a gay man in the 1960s and was too scared or ashamed to back out of it. My father *had sex with other men.*"

"I'm aware. I was at dinner too when Catherine told us all of this."

"Then why aren't you more freaked out? Why does everyone around me act like this was a perfectly fine and normal situation?" Dane let go of Olive's hand and put both of his hands in his hair, holding the sides of his head like his brain hurt.

Olive shrugged and looked around. "Because it *was* kind of normal," she said, her voice going up an octave. "Not in every family. But Dane, this was a time when people weren't free to be who they truly were. And I knew your parents. I saw them together—there was real love there. Maybe more friendship love than romantic love, but it was there. And there was respect. What they had is not our business, nor is it even relevant today. They're both gone. It's over."

Dane looked at her frantically. "But my real dad was just some guy and my mother isn't here anymore to answer my questions. How am I ever supposed to know who I am now?"

Olive went still. This was the moment to bring the man she'd married back to Earth and she knew it. "Dane," she said, feeling a huge cloud of calm settle over her. She'd held this information for long enough, knowing that it could possibly either help or hurt her husband. Olive kept her eyes locked on his as she spoke. "I've met with Catherine a number of times since all of this happened, and I have something I want to tell you. But you need to be ready for it, okay?"

Dane's face paled. There'd already been so much: finding out that his parents' relationship was a sham. Knowing that his dad had likely slept with men he knew in their small town—Dane's third grade teacher, who'd always been a little different; the man who'd lived on the corner and mowed his lawn shirtless, even in February; Mr. Akins who owned the corner store and gave free candy to any little boy who'd lift up their shirt and show him the smooth skin of their bellies. Dane shuddered now, imagining. And then the final nail in the coffin, quite literally: finding out that his father hadn't died from leukemia, but AIDS. It had all sent Dane into the kind of existential tailspin that it was nearly impossible to come out of.

Watching Dane's face, she wasn't sure he was ready, but Olive pushed ahead anyway. "Catherine found out before your mother passed that she'd specifically chosen the man she wanted to father her children—the children that she desperately wanted and that your father also desperately wanted." She stepped forward and put her arms around her husband's waist there on the front porch of a rundown biker's hangout on the outskirts of a town called Leith in a country far from their own. Where they were hardly mattered; what mattered was that she was going to give him what she saw as a gift, so she held him in her arms and looked up at his face. "Your mom and dad convinced your Uncle Paul to be the father of their children. Your dad's brother."

In that moment, Olive was glad to be holding him as he swayed slightly on his feet. It wasn't as though she could have done much had he really fainted—after all, Dane was about six inches taller than her and at least a hundred pounds heavier—but it still felt as though her touch might have some sort of soothing quality that would keep him on his feet.

"What?" Dane said quietly, looking completely stricken. "You mean...my mom and Uncle Paul..."

"Shh," Olive said, shaking her head firmly. "Who cares. Not

important," she said, watching him carefully. "The hows and whys don't matter. What matters is that you *are* related to your dad. He raised you. He loved you. He wanted you. There is absolutely *nothing* to be ashamed of when it comes to your family. Do you hear me?"

Dane blinked, still in shock. It took him several moments to get the words together that he wanted to say. Finally, he pulled away from Olive and sank down, sitting on the front step of the house. Olive looked around, wondering about the safety of just hanging out there at the house of a Scottish biker gang, but then again, she wasn't the one in shock; she'd had this information in her back pocket for over a year now, and it wasn't her family, so the impact wasn't the same.

She sat next to Dane and put a hand on his back, rubbing in slow circles just like she'd done for the kids when they were small. "You okay?"

Dane nodded and put his head into his hands. He didn't look at her. "Weirdly, yeah," he said, giving a small laugh that was buried in his big hands as they rubbed his tired face. "I guess it's all water under the bridge, huh? Nothing much to do about it but to figure out what that makes me."

"It makes you a person with a complicated family." Olive kept rubbing his back, letting her mind wander to her own weird, rambling family. "Just like everyone else."

"No," Dane said, lifting his head. He looked at her seriously. "That's not what I mean." There was the faintest glimmer of mirth in Dane's eyes as he looked at her. "What I meant was, what does that make me? Like, if my uncle is actually my father...am I my own cousin or something?"

Olive waited. To make a sudden move might be the wrong thing to do. But then, out of nowhere, Dane's face broke into a huge grin and the laugh she'd loved for years but hadn't heard for what felt like ages came bursting forth, making his entire upper body shake. Olive couldn't help it: she put her forehead to his shoulder and started to giggle. Soon, they were swatting at each other like a couple of teenagers, fighting off gales of laughter about the very thing that had caused Dane so much torment these past couple of years.

"Ollie," he finally said, letting his laugh subside. "This whole thing has really messed with my head. Do you understand?"

"I do. Of course I do. But you've got to figure out how to accept it without letting it decide who you are. Only *you* get to decide that. Not your parents, not their actions, none of it."

Dane nodded, looking thoughtful as he ran a hand over his chin and down his neck.

"Do you wish Catherine had never told you? Or that I'd kept this to myself?"

He thought about it. "I don't know, Ol. Knowing where we come from is a pretty big thing, but...I probably could have lived without the whole truth about my dad. I don't hate him for it, and obviously my mom was fine with it—or at least accepted it—but sometimes it's hard to reconcile someone's real self with the person you thought you knew."

Olive put her hand on his back again and rubbed his shoulder blades.

"And no, I'm glad you told me this. It kind of completes the puzzle." He was quiet for a second and then stood abruptly. "But I wasted so much time and energy on this, Olive. I screwed up everything because I freaked out. I thought my whole life was a lie."

"It's not," Olive said, shaking her head vehemently as she watched her husband. "The kids and I are exactly what you think we are. We're a solid foundation, Dane."

"I know. And I took that for granted while I locked myself into this mental hell," he said, tapping his forehead with the tips of all ten fingers. Dane held out a hand to Olive and pulled her up off the porch so that they were standing face to face. "And I'm sorry. I lost my job and had to start over, which put our family in jeopardy, and I shut you out. I can't even imagine what the kids think of me."

"They're adults now, so they probably think what all adult children do: that their parents are nutjobs who sprang forth fully formed from some prehistoric time, having never lived through adolescence." They chuckled together. "But truly, they love you, Dane. We all do, and all we've wanted was for you to accept your family, learn to love them for all their flaws, and feel whole again."

Dane's chin dropped and his eyes fell to the ground. On his face was a look of contrition. "I really mucked things up."

Olive shrugged and put her arms around him again. "So un-muck them," she said, looking up at the face of the man she'd loved for thirty years. They stared into one another's eyes for a moment and Dane was about to say something when the front door burst open, amplifying the already thumping bass of the music coming from inside. There were shouts and screams, and as Lucy, Edgar, and the three girls came running down the steps, empty beer bottles flew after them like missiles, shattering on the pavement at their feet.

Instinctively, Dane pulled Olive closer. "What the hell is going on here?" he shouted, reaching for the closest teenage girl and pushing her behind his back, also on instinct. "What is this?"

"Go, go!" Lucy said, taking Filene and Snow by the hands and motioning for Edgar to take Vanderbilt's hand and drag her along. All three girls looked completely puzzled as the adults surrounded them like a shield, shepherding them down the street.

They splashed through puddles and rounded a corner as a unit of interlocked hands, leaving the party well behind them as they turned onto a quiet street. The windows of the houses were dark, and a dog barked insistently from behind a fence, but they felt safer being out of view of the biker house.

"Okay," Dane said, huffing a little as he caught his breath, both hands on his hips. "What the hell is going on? We found these girls and—good lord, what happened?" His face was a mask of shock as he looked at Snow and finally took in her appearance.

The black tights she'd worn under her short black dress were shredded, and streams of blood ran down the bare skin that now showed up and down her thighs. Her red lipstick and black eyeliner was smeared like a little girl whose mother had come home and wiped off the evidence of an ill-fated attempt at putting on makeup, and her tears ran in dirty rivulets down both cheeks. One strap of her dress had been cut and was hanging down, revealing a triangle of black lacy bra. Dane looked away.

The other two girls didn't look much better, though their clothing was intact and other than some smeared makeup from their tears, they appeared physically unharmed.

"I'm calling us a taxi if I can't get an Uber," Edgar said, stepping away from the group slightly to figure out how to get them back into the city as quickly as possible.

The dog behind the fence continued to bark at the strange humans invading its space. Lucy shushed it as Snow began to sob openly, the shock finally hitting her. Filene and Snow huddled around her, holding her between them.

With a sigh, Lucy watched them. "Snow got herself into a real situation," she said, finally turning to look at Dane and Olive. "And incidentally, thanks for coming out here as back up," she added.

"We didn't do anything, but we're glad to be here," Olive said.

"I just..." Lucy shook her head and rubbed both temples. "I can't imagine what would have happened if we hadn't shown up."

"Bad things were already happening," Filene said angrily, though it wasn't clear exactly who she was angry at—the bikers, her friends, herself. "Snow was on the bed—" her voice hitched and she stopped, unable to say it out loud.

"Snow was tied to the bed by her wrists and ankles," Lucy said, employing her well-honed forensic pathologist's ability to report facts about horrific things while placing her own feelings in a box to deal with later. "Two men were on the bed, cutting her clothes off slowly with large knives."

Olive sucked in a breath loudly, her hand flying to her mouth. "No," she whispered.

"And two other men had taken Vanderbilt and Filene and were tying them to chairs so they'd be forced to watch."

"They pulled my hair," Vanderbilt said softly, putting a hand to her scalp tenderly. She looked more like an eight-year-old in that moment than a young woman on the cusp of adulthood. Her eyes welled with tears.

"Thank god we got there when we did," Lucy said, her eyes burning hotly as she looked at each girl in turn. "I know for a fact that these men weren't just playing a game of cat and mouse with the girls, this would not have ended with them simply being let go. It was an extremely dangerous scene, and I think we got there just in time."

Snow's sobs had turned to chest-heaving sniffles. She buried her face in Filene's shoulder.

Edgar came back to the group with his phone in one hand. "Uber will be here in minutes," he said. "Directly back to the hotel, or do we need to talk to the police?"

Lucy turned to Dane. "Did you ever get ahold of your friend at Police Scotland?"

"I had a call in to him when you texted Olive, so we came right over. No return call yet."

"Then let's head back to the hotel and wait to hear from him. When we do, I think we need to file a report immediately. This could have ended much worse than it did."

Snow's sobs started up again and Filene put an arm around her as the van that Edgar ordered pulled up next to them.

Within the hour, Lucy had the girls tucked away safely in their room, a pot of tea delivered to them, and the promise extracted from Filene that she'd call her—no matter the hour—if they needed her. Olive and Dane had retired to their room (looking quite a bit more hands-on with one another than Lucy remembered) with the assurance that they'd also call or text Lucy if they heard from Police Scotland, and Lucy found herself sitting in the tiny hotel bar next to Edgar, waiting for the handlebar mustached bartender to pour them each two fingers of Scotch.

"This is quite the joint, isn't it?" Lucy said, lifting her glass to Edgar and leaning her elbows on the bar as she glanced around the small room.

She'd yet to have a drink here, but wasn't surprised to find that the bar was just like the rest of the hotel: made of a lot of wood, covered with plaid curtains, and filled with paintings of ducks and fish. There were five stools running the length of the polished bar top, and two small tables near a window.

Edgar's eyes swept the room. "It's cozy, I suppose. In a 'I like to spend rainy weekends in the woods with a bunch of men trying to kill animals' sort of way."

Lucy laughed and felt the first sip of Scotch warm her cold insides. "So that's not you, huh, Edgar? You didn't grow up hunting with your dad?"

Edgar set his glass on the bar and focused on the wood for a long beat. "Nope. Not that kind of childhood. I grew up entirely in the city, just me, my mom, my sister, and my superheroes. Probably would've helped me if I had grown up with a dad doing that kind of stuff, you know?"

Lucy's mouth turned down as she watched Edgar's shoulders roll forward into a self-protective hunch.

"Hey, no," she said, leaning over and bumping his shoulder with her own. "You're great just the way you are. I mean that."

Edgar chuckled sarcastically. "Yes, being a balding bachelor in his fifties who loves comics and superheroes is pretty amazing. You would be amazed at how many women are into that."

Lucy wasn't sure how to respond. It was true: she probably wouldn't want to date a guy who thought he was a caped crusader, but it didn't mean that she didn't think Edgar was appealing in his own way. Kind, funny, easy to be around. She was already picturing how he could market himself on a dating app when he spoke again.

"I had a girl once," he said, taking a drink of Scotch and looking at the dark window with longing, like he might find this woman standing there, staring back at him.

"She liked me for me, and I definitely liked her for her," he said, a smile pulling at the corner of his mouth. "But her parents disapproved, and that mattered to her. She was first generation Chinese-American and we met at work, but ultimately her parents had the final say." He looked at Lucy sadly. "We were young—maybe twenty-two—so when they decided to move to California, she went with them, of course. And this was in the days before social media and the internet, so tracking her down was nearly impossible."

"Have you given it any thought? It's not impossible anymore."

Edgar's eyebrows shot up. "Have I thought about finding Carol?"

"Yeah. The world is totally connected, Edgar. We could probably look her up now and find at least something about her."

He finished his Scotch and motioned to the bartender to please pour another. "To think we could be sitting here in Scotland, trying to find a woman I haven't seen or heard from in more than thirty years." He shook his head and pushed his glass forward so the bartender could refill it. "That's amazing."

"I've never been a huge user of social media," Lucy admitted. "I was always busy with work and didn't care too much about updating people on everything I did, but since starting The Holiday Adventure Club, I've grown much more adept." She reached into her purse, which was hanging over the back of her chair, and pulled out her phone. "Just say the word."

Edgar was looking at her dubiously. "I don't know...won't that be an invasion of privacy? Looking up someone who maybe doesn't want to be found?"

"Everyone is out there, Edgar. If she's alive, she has a digital footprint of some sort."

"If she's alive," he said, letting his chin drop. He nodded sadly. "That is a big if. We're in our fifties—any number of things could have happened at this point."

Lucy set her phone on the bar and swung her knees around so that she was facing Edgar. "Let's not think like that," she said. "I was a doctor long enough to know the kinds of things that befall people in middle age, and I've seen most of it with my own eyes, but I say we look at this as a mini-adventure here on your big adventure to Scotland."

Edgar laughed again. "Well, it has been full of adventure. The old guy nearly drowning. The girls tonight."

"God," Lucy said, putting a hand on Edgar's sleeve. "Tonight was so overwhelming that I totally forgot about the guy who almost drowned at Jupiter Artland."

"I never forget a single person whose life I interact with in that way."

"You mean the people you save?" Lucy kept her hand on his sleeve as she looked at him, hoping her intense gaze would bring him around.

"Oh, I think 'save' is a strong word," Edgar said modestly. "I just happen to be in the right place at the right time."

"Okay, then maybe Carol needs you to be in the right place at the right time. Who's to say she isn't in need of someone reaching out to her right now?"

Edgar turned his head just enough so that they were looking one another in the eye. "I don't know about that. And I'm terrified to find out bad news about her."

"What's the worst news? That she's married? A grandmother?"

"No," Edgar said, his voice dull and flat. "That she didn't make it. That she's gone. If she was a married grandmother I'd be *thrilled*. She was a wonderful girl and she deserved all the happiness that life has to offer. I would sleep better knowing that she was safe and living a full life."

"Then I guess that's your answer," Lucy said, letting go of his arm and waving a hand in the air. "But it's also the gamble you'd be taking —is she safe and happy? Or is there bad news out there?"

Edgar nodded and sipped his Scotch quietly. Lucy kept her mouth shut and let him process. She had no idea why, at the end of an exhaustingly long day and a dramatic evening, she wanted to delve into Edgar's past and hunt down a woman he hadn't seen since his twenties, but for some reason she felt giddy at the idea of unearthing something good.

Lord, she said to herself, *please let us find something good.*

Finally, Edgar took off his glasses and set them on the bar, rubbing his eyes with both hands. He turned to Lucy. "Okay, let's look her up."

"Yes!" Lucy exclaimed, clapping her hands. The bartender glanced their way from over the top of a dog-eared book that he held in one hand. They were the only patrons in the bar. "Sorry," she mouthed to him, but he merely shrugged and went back to his book.

"Let's do this," Lucy said. She unlocked her phone and opened Facebook. "We'll start in the obvious place, but with the under-standing that there might be hundreds of women with her name."

Edgar sighed loudly. "Got it. She went by Carol, but her real first name was Lian—that means 'graceful willow,' which she was." He looked into the distance dreamily. "Her last name was Huang."

Lucy quickly tried combinations of the names: Carol Huang. Lian Huang. Lian Carol Huang. They hunched over the phone on the bar, scrolling through the images of women who shared the name of the girl Edgar once loved.

"Maybe?" he'd say, pointing hesitantly at a profile picture and waiting for Lucy to open it. Then, brows furrowed, eyes serious: "No, that's not her. At least I don't think so."

After a few minutes Lucy opened an internet browser and went to a person finder site, typing in all the same info. "What year would you say she was born, approximately?"

"We're the same age, so 1968."

Lucy put that information in. "And we know she lived in New York City because that's where you said you were living in your twenties, right?"

"Good memory," Edgar said, looking surprised. "And her family moved to San Francisco, so I know two places she's lived."

They added that information and hit "search."

There were seventeen hits.

"This is way more manageable than combing through hundreds of women on Facebook without anything else to go on. Let's peek at these ladies," Lucy said.

Together, they clicked each woman, easily ruling out fourteen of them based on dates of birth.

"Three," Edgar said, looking at the names on the screen. "Now what?"

"Now we go back to Facebook and put in these cities along with the names," Lucy said, tapping her finger on the screen where the women's current addresses were. One was in San Francisco, one in Seattle, and another in a small town called Avalon, California.

Edgar rubbed his hands together nervously. "I'm ready."

Lucy gave him a second to make sure he really was ready, then she went back to Facebook and narrowed down their search by location.

Carol Huang from San Francisco appeared on the screen. She had dark hair, a bright smile, and was surrounded by little girls with ink black hair. They clicked through a few photos that were available for anyone on Facebook to see and Edgar shook his head. "No," he said. "This lady looks happy and I'd be glad to see Carol living this life, but that's not her. She had this, like, scar on her chin. It wasn't very visible, but up close you could see it. Even in this photo," he said, pointing at the close-up profile picture, "there's no scar. Not her."

They moved on to the next woman—the one from Avalon. Her smile was sad and it said she was divorced in her profile. The full-length photo of her convinced Edgar immediately that this was not his Carol. "Next," he said, sounding like he was losing hope.

They clicked on the woman from Seattle. A widow. Several family photos including what appeared to be grown children and even grandchildren. Pictures of her sitting in a chair at Christmas next to a tree, laughter on her face as she opened a gift. More photos of her in the kitchen cooking, pointing a spatula at a laughing man who must have been her son.

And finally, a close-up photo. The faintest scar on her soft chin.

Edgar inhaled sharply. "This is her. This is my Carol."

Lucy felt warmth blooming in her chest. *My Carol*, he'd said. She smiled. "This is her?"

Edgar nodded, lips pressed together, eyes shining. "It's her," he whispered, leaning on his elbows as he looked more closely. "It's definitely her."

Lucy put an arm around his broad shoulders. "What should we do? Do you want to message her? I'm assuming you have Facebook—you could send her a friend request and surely she'd see your name and remember instantly who you are."

Edgar looked at Lucy with eyes full of the kind of hope and expectation and unbridled fear that people feel when they're poised on the edge of a cliff in life, ready to take a big leap. "You think I should?"

Lucy weighed the question. Of course she thought he should, or she never would have brought up the idea of tracking down Carol. But she also knew that these were people's lives, not just fictional characters in a book she was reading. However, Edgar was single, and Carol's profile said that she was a widow and offered no photos of her with any other men who didn't appear to be her sons or, perhaps, nephews, so it seemed like no harm would be done. The worst thing would be if she rejected or ignored his request. Or maybe didn't remember him. But life was full of possibilities...roads not taken... regrets. And though she'd known Edgar for only a short time, she didn't want him to go on living with any regret. At least not over this.

"Yes," Lucy said firmly, giving a single nod. "I think you should."

Before he could stop himself, Edgar pulled his own phone out of his coat pocket, opened Facebook, searched for the woman whose face was still smiling at them from Lucy's screen, and clicked on her.

He stopped with his finger poised over the "Add Friend" button. "Should I? You're sure?"

Lucy nodded. "I'm sure. Go for it, Edgar."

So he did.

"Sent!" he crowed with gusto, looking around as if he expected the empty bar to explode into applause. "Holy cow, I found Carol. Well, you found Carol. I can't believe this. What do we do now? All these years and she's out there. Alive. Looking as beautiful as ever." Edgar stood up from the tall bar chair and paced back and forth, looking shell-shocked. "It's still early in the day there. Do you think she'll accept? What should I do while I wait?"

Lucy turned in her chair, arm resting on the back of it as she watched Edgar with amusement. Even the bartender had put down his book and was watching, looking somewhat invested, as he'd certainly heard the entire conversation, given their close proximity in the small space.

Lucy stood up, pulled some bills from her purse, and laid them on the bar. "I think we should try to get some sleep," she said, putting a hand on Edgar's arm to slow his pacing. "Nothing to do now but wait."

"Sleep?" Edgar said, stopping in his tracks. He shook his head. "I can't sleep, Lucy. I'm too keyed up."

Lucy laughed. "Well, friend, I have to get some sleep. This day has been full of far more adventure than I'm used to, and I think I'm about to turn into a pumpkin here."

Edgar ran both hands through his salt-and-pepper hair and left it standing on end. "Okay, okay. You sleep. I'll tell you as soon as I hear something, okay? I'll tell you right away. And Lucy? Thanks."

Lucy laughed again, but more softly. "You're welcome. But I do hope you get some sleep, Edgar. Try, will you?"

Edgar nodded at her distractedly, already sliding into his seat at the bar and looking ready for a long night ahead. "For sure. I will," he promised, not sounding like he would at all.

Lucy smiled at his back as she walked through the door of the bar and into the lobby. As she made her way tiredly down the hallway to her room she put her phone on mute. Between Edgar and the girls who were hopefully fast asleep in their own room, it was far too likely that someone might send her a message and wake her up, and all Lucy needed right then was about seven hours of completely uninterrupted sleep.

Chapter 12

April 17

Edinburgh

Lucy counted heads as the group huddled together outside a rickety-looking stone building: nineteen, including herself. It was nearly pitch black outside, with just one streetlight nearby to cast a glow on the wet cobblestones.

"I'm scared," Vanderbilt whispered, holding both Snow and Filene's hands. The girls had appeared that morning at breakfast looking wizened by their experience the night before. With some serious talk, Lucy had agreed to not call their parents to alert them to the near-miss with the bikers, but there was a part of her that thought she'd possibly like to know about it if she were a mother. But then again, maybe not. Everyone survived their own youthful stupidity somehow, and her only immediate job was to keep her eyes on the girls. They'd made it easy for her all day, sticking close to Lucy through a visit to the Scottish National Galleries—something she'd have never expected them to agree to prior to their scary night on the town.

Edgar stood to the side, hands in the pockets of his windbreaker, a dazed smile on his face. He'd been waiting for Lucy in the lobby of the hotel when she got back from the museum with the small group that had joined her, and the second he'd spotted her he'd shouted her name.

"Lucy! Guess what?"

Lucy had stopped in her tracks, afraid of another crisis of any sort. So far Edinburgh had been rife with a couple on the verge of collapse, a man who'd nearly drowned right under their noses, and three young ladies who'd come far too close to knives and danger for her comfort. All she wanted now was a trip to the National museum, a little more shopping on Victoria Street, and a night out with the group taking a Haunted Edinburgh guided tour, which they were about to embark upon.

"Carol answered!" Edgar had shouted across the lobby, his voice echoing and causing heads to turn. "She said yes to my friend request!"

Lucy had excused herself from the others and promised the girls that she'd see them after dinner for the haunted tour, then sat down with Edgar to get the whole story. The short version of his very excited, rambling, detail-rich tale was that she'd seen his request, accepted it, and sent him a message inviting him to tell her how he was doing and how he'd found her after all these years. After ordering a pot of tea, Lucy and Edgar had sat in the lobby for another hour and a half crafting a perfect response and then sending it, much to Edgar's extreme joy and anticipation.

Now, he stood amongst them, ready for this evening tour but clearly with his head in the clouds. Lucy smiled at him as he looked around, most likely thinking of Carol and not of which stranger he might need to save next.

"Is this the Holiday Adventure Club?" a young woman asked, walking toward them with a clipboard.

"Yes," Lucy called out, raising her hand in the air. "I'm Lucy."

Their tour guide was about six inches shorter than Lucy and with a smattering of freckles across her small nose. Her bright red hair was pulled into two cute puffs above her ears, which held a mixture of dainty gold studs and hoops.

"I'm Ella," she said in a British accent. The name tag affixed to her navy blue jacket confirmed this, along with her hometown, which was London. "I'd love to take you under the city and tell you all about the witches and ghosts who live amongst us and sleep beneath our feet here in Edinburgh. Are we ready?" She smiled brightly, like the tour was going to be about spring flowers and sunshine rather than murder and mystery.

Ella led them through the door of a shop and then down a dank, narrow stone staircase to a hallway that smelled of moss and decay.

"Edinburgh is extremely well-known for body snatching," the tiny redhead said, inserting a giant skeleton key into a rusty lock and twisting until the wooden door gave way with a creak on its hinges. "Two famous body snatchers went by the names Burke and Hare, and they would creep about in the night, acquiring dead bodies for the famous physicians of the day like Dr. Knox."

Olive scooted closer to Dane and slipped her hand into his, squeezing it.

"They got caught because their desire to find bodies led them to catching 'fresh' ones rather than just digging them out of the dirt like normal grave-robbers."

Lucy wrapped her arms around herself, wishing she had a hand to hold, but not feeling the least bit afraid. A dead body here or there wouldn't throw her; she'd done her time alone in a room with the nearly and dearly departed, and more than anything, this tour was going to be a point of interest—hopefully with some interesting facts or minor scares.

"Along the path here you'll see candles lit, so watch yourself and don't get too close to the flames, please," Ella said, pointing around the damp vault with both hands like a flight attendant showing her passengers where the exit doors were. "And overhead you'll see stalactites formed by the city's dregs, so don't look up, or you might get an eyeful of that!"

"Ewww," Snow whispered, her voice echoing and bouncing around off the stone walls. "What are dregs?"

Lucy glanced back to see the girls all walking arm-in-arm.

"It's like all the gross stuff off the streets that's soaked through and collected there. Mud and dirt and sludge and anything nasty you can think of," Filene said.

Snow made a gagging sound.

"Everywhere you go in Edinburgh you're likely to encounter a wee bit of paranormal activity," Ella went on, walking backwards as she talked to the group. "And nowhere is quite so well known for its ghostly goings on as right here, beneath the city."

A collective "ooohhhh" rose up from the group as they followed Ella.

For the next hour and a half, they took digital photos in hopes of catching images of blobs and spirits, listened to stories of death and witchery, and then ended the tour with a ride on a black bus once used to transport dead bodies. The bus dropped them in a graveyard for a final scare.

Lucy loved all of it, and as she watched the faces of her new friends and travel companions, she realized that they did too. It was a perfect distraction from the drama of the night before, and while some of the stories actually were a little spooky, none of it compared to the fear Lucy had felt seeing Snow battered and bleeding. She gave a final shudder at the memory of that and packed it away in her mind.

Edgar had teamed up on the tour with a trio of what appeared to be Comic Con participants, dressed as they were in various super-hero-type costumes and makeup. The man Edgar was talking to at the edge of the graveyard was about twenty years younger than he, and dressed in a fitted red, blue, and gold leather jacket with stars all over it, though Lucy had no idea who he was supposed to be dressed as. His sandy hair was brushed to one side, and from his hip hung a sword that was obviously plastic. The two women he'd come on the tour with swept around the graveyard in black sequined cloaks and eye masks, posing for photos with ancient headstones and looking serious as they discussed the possibility that the specters of the long dead might appear in their photos. Lucy shook her head; these people were fully committed to their cause—she had to give them that.

As she reached into her purse to find her phone so that she could snap a photo of the graveyard (at Ella's encouragement—she promised that most people ended up with an orb or two in the picture when they did that), Lucy found that it was already buzzing. She pulled it out with a frown and glanced at the screen. It was a message from her aunt Sharon.

Please don't worry, love, but your mom vanished on me today. The police found her in the parking lot at the grocery store asking people for money and they brought her home. Everything is FINE though, Lucy. She's okay!!!

Lucy read the message three times before her heart started beating again. She put her phone back into her purse with shaking hands and looked around to find that everyone was congregating near the bus again for the ride back to the hotel.

The grocery store parking lot? Begging for money? Vanished? A sense of horror washed over Lucy as she realized that maybe her aunt Sharon wasn't capable of managing her mother anymore. That maybe she'd made a huge mistake leaving Buffalo and planning a year of adventure while her mother slowly lost her bearings in this world.

A gust of wind blew through the graveyard then, sending the leaves on the trees above into a frenzy of activity like wind chimes in a storm. She looked up and watched the dark foliage overhead, feeling a sense of foreboding and dread that had nothing to do with the fact that she was in an old graveyard at midnight.

Lucy shoved her hands into the pockets of her coat and walked around the stones set flat into the grass, giving the dead the respect of not stepping directly on their graves.

It was time to get home. Time to assess this situation further. Time to get her real life squared away.

Chapter 13

April 21
Amelia Island, FL

April brought with it the kind of rapidly increasing warmth that bathed Florida in heat until at least October. Most of the snowbirds had packed up and fled back to more temperate climes, and everyone left to bake under the hot sun ambled about in shorts and sleeveless shirts, tanned skin on full display as they walked the beach, swam in the pools inside their gated condominium communities, and ate dinner on the porches of restaurants all over Amelia Island.

Nick had greeted Lucy with a sweeping hug the minute she'd appeared on his doorstep, which was the first thing she did upon arriving home.

"Hi!" Nick said, scooping her up and holding her close. "I missed you."

Lucy buried her face in his neck and inhaled his scent sharply. She'd missed him too, but heavy on her mind was the feeling that she was saddling this man—this sweet, creative, funny, kind man—with her own baggage. The entire flight home she'd fretted about her mother and what to do about her increasing level of need, about whether it was even prudent to leave the country once a month for the rest of the year, and about whether she was an asset or a liability to Nick.

Sure, they both had their "stuff"—Nick losing a child to cancer, as she'd found out on their trip to St. Barts—definitely qualified as "stuff," but a part of Lucy felt like damaged goods. *She* was the one who couldn't get pregnant when she and Jason had tried. *She* was the one who wasn't good enough to keep the husband who'd promised to love and hold her until death parted them. *She* was the one who'd fled to Amelia Island and immediately ran into the arms of a blockhead named Charlie.

But instead of saying any of those things, Lucy lifted her head from Nick's shoulder and looked him in the eye. "I missed you too," she said, smiling as he kissed her there on his front porch. Behind him, Hemingway sat obediently, tail swishing across the hardwood floor just inside the entryway as he watched his master bestow affection upon another human.

"And Hemmie," Lucy said, pulling away from Nick and falling to her knees. "I missed you just as much!" Hearing his name, the dog jumped up and came to her, putting his black head on her knee and waiting to be petted and told what a good boy he was.

Nick opened the door all the way and offered Lucy a hand to pull her up. "Come in," he said. "Can you stay?"

Lucy looked out at her car in the driveway. The sun was still low in the sky; it wasn't even nine o'clock in the morning yet.

"Stay?" she asked, smiling at him as Hemingway ran through the house and disappeared out the dog door into the back yard.

"It's Sunday," Nick said with a shrug.

"You're right. It is. And yes, I'd love to stay." Lucy put her hands on both sides of his waist and stood up on her toes to kiss him again. "I'd love to stay as long as you'll have me."

Nick brushed her hair from her eyes and kissed the tip of her nose as he closed the door to the world outside.

* * *

Later that evening, Nick and Lucy walked along the beach together, holding hands and talking.

"Are you excited for Morocco?" he asked.

Lucy looked over at him and was reminded of their walk on the beach on St. Barts. "Yeah, I am," she said, but her words came out haltingly. "It's just...my mom. My aunt Sharon said she went missing a few days ago and we've talked on the phone about thirty-seven times to make sure we have a foolproof plan so that it won't happen again, but there's no guarantee."

"Okay. Let's talk. What systems do you have in place?"

Lucy held up her free hand and started ticking items off on her fingers. "We got a security system installed so that any door or window sets off a small alarm when it's opened. We're ordering a fence that runs the perimeter of the property and has a gate with a keypad on it. She won't ever know the code, so essentially that should keep her close to the house if she ever does get out."

Nick tipped his head from side to side as he listened. "So far it sounds solid. What's missing?"

Lucy dragged her foot along the wet sand as they walked, making a trail behind her the way a little kid might. "Uhhh, I don't know. Something though. I can't put my finger on it."

Nick stayed quiet as they walked. Instead of speaking, he squeezed her hand once, twice, three times. The sky was a trail of pink across the evening's darkening blues and Lucy watched the sun blazing its way to the horizon.

"I think it's me," Lucy finally said. "I think I have to close up shop and go back there and do what I'm supposed to do. Be a daughter. Live there. Put my own life on hold—"

"Now wait just a second." Nick stopped walking but kept holding her hand. The ocean washed onto the shore and then retreated behind him as he turned to look at Lucy. "I'm not saying this purely for selfish reasons, but your life is here. You clearly chose to come to Florida, to open a new business, and to do something that you'd never done before. You're ensuring that she has care up there, and you go to visit as often as you can. No one can ask for more than that."

"*Everyone* can ask for more than that," Lucy said, feeling her face heat up. "You have no idea because you're a man. I'm sorry, but it's true." She let go of his hand and ran her fingers through her hair in frustration. "People definitely expect the adult daughter to do the heavy lifting when it comes to aging parents. And I'm rebelling against that just a little, which is incredibly difficult to do."

"So if you were a son, this wouldn't even be a question?"

"Not as much. I could go anywhere and do anything and just pay the bills. But I guarantee there are people who would read the story of my life and think, 'Wow. Selfish girl. Leaving her mother like that.'"

"Well I don't think that."

"Yeah, but you're you. And you clearly believe that women have lives outside of being caregivers to parents and children and husbands. We're allowed to make choices too."

Nick nodded and then reached out with both hands, pulling her close to him. Lucy sighed as she wrapped her arms around him and pressed her face to his chest.

"Hell yeah, you're allowed," Nick whispered into her hair. "You can do anything you set your mind to."

"There just isn't enough time to do it all, Nick."

He pulled away from her, but kept his hands on both of her shoulders as he looked her in the eye. "I have an idea," Nick said. "How about if I go up there and meet Aunt Sharon, check out the new system, and see if there's anything else that needs to be done to keep Mom safe? I mean, you need to be in Morocco in a week, so I can definitely do this for you. I'll fly up over a weekend and—"

"Nick," Lucy stopped him, dropping her gaze to the sand. "That's so nice, but I can't ask you to do that. We just barely started...dating? Is that what you'd call this at our age?"

"Number one, you're not asking me, I'm offering," Nick clarified. "I want to help you. And number two, we don't need to define anything. We're seeing each other. We're happy. But I can easily go up there as a concerned friend and offer my help and opinions. Nothing weird about that."

Lucy thought about it. It *did* sound nice to have someone else step in and offer their thoughts and assistance after so many years of doing it on her own. She sometimes forgot to give herself credit for how long she'd been her mother's primary caregiver. Mind you, it was agoraphobia she'd grappled with for over twenty years and the dementia was a more recent development, but all told, Lucy had been on the front lines since she was only sixteen, and frankly, she was exhausted.

She relented. "You'd do that for me? What about the shop?"

"I'd definitely do it for you, and I'd fly up on a Friday night, close the shop on Saturday, and be back by Monday morning to open it again. Or if not, I'd close it on Monday too. I don't know, but that's not your concern. I can arrange it all."

"Nick..." Lucy tried to think of a good argument but came up empty-handed. It wasn't in her nature to admit that she needed help, so this was hard. She chewed on her lower lip for a minute, considering all the possible pitfalls and obstacles. Other than Aunt Sharon and Nick not knowing one another yet, or her mom being confused by a handsome stranger showing up instead of her daughter, there really were none. "I can't believe you'd go up there for me."

"Believe it. I will. I'll go on Friday, since you're leaving on Sunday and will probably be packing and prepping all weekend. That way if anything goes wrong, you're still here and I can reach you quickly and easily. How does that sound?"

"That honestly sounds amazing. And so helpful." Lucy put her hands over her face and breathed in and out a few times. "I just have so much to do." She gave a sad little laugh. "This isn't the first time that I've asked myself what the hell I was thinking planning all these trips in one year."

Nick shrugged. "Must've been something you felt you needed to do. I'm all for it. Just as long as you don't fall in love with Tangier or Casablanca and never come back."

Lucy took her hands from her eyes and looked at Nick, laughing for real this time. "I think staying in Morocco is a long shot. I'll be back on May 9th and then I *promise* I'll be here for a while. The next trip isn't until July."

Nick blew out a breath, nodding. "I'm looking forward to that. Just a stretch of time when we can do normal couple things. Make dinner, watch movies, come to the beach for an evening stroll." He took her hand again and they started walking again. "I'm an easygoing guy, and I want a gal like you by my side. I'm happy to support your travels, but I'm not gonna lie: I miss you."

"Hey," Lucy said, putting her free hand into the pocket of her shorts as they walked. She suddenly felt shy, in spite of the fact that they'd spent most of the day in Nick's bed together. "I *really* miss you. When I called you from that science convention, I wanted to see your face, but I knew if I FaceTimed you it might make me cry."

"Awww! No!" Nick laughed, but in a way that showed how flattered he was. A seagull spotted something just ahead of them and swooped in to inspect the possible treat, tucking its wings in as it pecked at a shell. "Don't cry, Lucy."

She felt a little embarrassed at her admission. Of course she missed Nick—he was her friend, her confidante, and currently the man in her life—but she also missed what he represented, which was familiarity, consistency, and home. And her travels were the polar opposite of all three of those things.

"It's all good." Lucy smiled at him confidently, intentionally turning up the wattage on her grin a few notches. "I've got this. And I appreciate you going up to Buffalo more than I can ever say."

"Not a problem," Nick assured her. "But let's talk about the details later." He steered her away from the water and toward the path that led up to the street. "Right now, all I want is ice cream."

"Yes!" Lucy said, tugging at his hand and feeling relief that the serious moment between them had passed. "Nothing better on a Sunday evening than ice cream."

Chapter 14

April 21

San Diego, CA

The beach house was completely open to the elements. Olive stood in the kitchen, barefoot, cutting cheese and placing crackers, salted nuts, dried fruits, stuffed olives, and jam on a giant charcuterie board.

"Hey, Mom?" Melody called out, walking into the open living space with a towel around her neck. "I'm going swimming."

Olive looked up at her daughter and smiled. She breathed in deeply, taking in the salty air that came through the open windows. The sliding glass door was open to a wooden deck covered with chaise lounges and a table with an umbrella and eight chairs. It was the perfect house to rent for a giant family gathering.

"Okay, hon," Olive said, standing still as Melody passed behind her, leaned in to put a kiss on her cheek, and stole a piece of sharp cheddar to eat on her way to the water. "Be careful. Who's going with you?"

"Mack," she said simply, walking through the sliding door and striding across the deck and down the sand. As Olive watched, sure enough, twelve-year-old Mack, her son Hunter's stepchild, raced after Melody with his long, gangly legs and floppy adolescent hair. Again, Olive smiled.

The second floor of the house was completely filled: Hunter and his wife and her boy Mack; Melody; Jack and his fiancée Kate; April and her girlfriend Prianka. They'd even invited Dane's sister Catherine and her family, and Olive had been thrilled when she'd accepted. She knew this was an important step for Dane, just moving ahead, finding a new normal. Accepting that Catherine had been the bearer of bad news, yes, but that maybe knowing was better than *not* knowing.

The whole mini-vacation had been a somewhat impromptu thing, planned by Olive from Edinburgh and pieced together by April and Catherine, and the three women had puzzled endlessly over the wisdom of their final move, which they'd finally agreed on unanimously: they'd invited Uncle Paul. He now knew that both Catherine and Dane were aware of the complex role he'd played in their origins, and while he'd been somewhat hesitant to have this first meet-up be at a family gathering, Olive had been sure that the ability to take a long walk on the beach or to find a quiet place in the giant rental house to talk would be far more conducive to this meeting than a dark bar or a nice restaurant.

Catherine's eighteen-year-old daughter walked through the house first, having just breezed through the front door without knocking.

"Aunt Olive!" she said, walking straight over and putting her long arms around her aunt's neck. Olive put down her knife and embraced the young girl.

"Hi, Kent," she said, stepping back and looking at her niece, who seemed to have grown four inches, lost all traces of teenage pudginess, and taken on a worldly air in less than a year. "You look gorgeous, honey."

Just then, Catherine and her husband and their son walked in together, and Olive smiled at her nephew as he walked and played his Nintendo Switch seamlessly, never breaking his stride or his eye contact with the game.

After them lumbered Uncle Paul, looking every bit the eighty-three year old man he was. His white hair was soft and tufted on his shiny scalp, face shaved smooth to reveal the folds of skin that would otherwise be hidden by a beard.

"Hello, darling," Paul said, walking straight to Olive and putting his rough hands on both sides of her face. He planted a kiss on her forehead. "Thank you for this." Already, his rheumy eyes were watery and in them Olive saw—not fear—apprehension? "I've been waiting a long time to have this discussion. Wasn't sure the day would ever come."

"Well, it has," Olive said gently, putting her hands on his elbows and then letting go as Dane walked into the room.

There was a moment of silence amongst the adults where eye contact was made fleetingly and questioningly. Catherine's son Jett continued to play his handheld game, wandering straight through the open door to the deck, and Kent followed on her long, bare legs, hair swinging across her back as she pulled her phone from the back pocket of her denim shorts and snagged a cracker on her way past the kitchen island.

Finally, they were alone. Catherine, Dane, Olive, Catherine's husband Ethan, and Uncle Paul. Olive and Ethan locked eyes and made a silent agreement to slip away. Though they'd both been a part of the family for decades, this wasn't their family drama to unfold.

"Wait," Dane said as Olive and Ethan tried to pick up a bottle of wine and two glasses and follow the kids out to the deck. "I want you guys here. I've put Olive through hell the past couple of years, and she deserves to hear everything, as does Ethan, I believe."

Olive and Ethan looked at one another quizzically; to be honest, she'd been looking forward to sitting outside in the afternoon sun and watching Melody and Mack play in the ocean just down the beach.

"If you're sure," Ethan said hesitantly, setting the wine glass back on the counter.

"I am," Dane said. "And I'm ready to hear everything, Uncle Paul. This has been a long fifty years for you—more than fifty years—

and ultimately you gave my parents a generous gift, and followed it up with yet another generous gift of silence for the rest of their lives."

Uncle Paul looked around for a place to sit and Olive realized that perhaps he was unsteady on his feet. Catherine spotted it too and quickly led him to the couch and got him settled. Everyone else sank into a chair or sat on the edge of the empty fireplace to listen.

"I'm ready," Uncle Paul said, clearing his throat. He paused for a long moment, gathering his thoughts as he knotted his liver-spotted hands together anxiously. It was clear that he'd been holding this in for so long that he wasn't sure he was ready to let it go. "Your parents met in the 60s, a much different time than the one we live in now," he began, looking up and meeting each of their eyes in turn with a firm, steady gaze. "But no matter what you hear me say today, please never forget that love is love, and what your parents had for one another *was* love, just in a different form than what people expected at that time."

As Uncle Paul spoke, Olive caught Dane's eye. For the first time in as long as she could remember, he looked open. Curious. Maybe even somewhat peaceful. She didn't want to get her hopes up, but in the days since they'd finally talked outside the biker house in Scotland (did she really just think those words in her head so casually? *Outside the biker house in Scotland*...this made her nearly chuckle out loud), he'd been so much like the old Dane she'd known and loved that her heart had been filled with hope.

As Olive looked at her husband now—he sitting next to his uncle on the couch, she perched on the edge of the cold, stone fireplace, just listening—he met her eye and held it. Just as she thought he'd look away, he mouthed three words to her that made her heart leap with joy:

I love you.

Chapter 15

April 22

Seattle, WA

It had taken all of Edgar's willpower to fly home from Edinburgh and get things settled in New York before racing across the country to Seattle to see Carol for the first time in thirty years.

He'd arrived at JFK already feeling the pulse of energy that comes with anticipation. He and Carol had been exchanging messages non-stop for days, catching up on their respective lives, and talking about the randomness of the universe. Edgar firmly believed that were it not for that drink with Lucy at the bar, he might've gone his entire life not doing a deep dive to find the woman who'd gotten away. He'd have lived out his remaining years and decades with her as a ghost, a faded image in a photo in his mind, wishing her well and wistfully thinking about what their lives together *could* have been.

But now. Now he'd found her, and that was all thanks to Lucy Landish and her insistence that they give it a shot. He owed her a debt of gratitude already, even if the only thing that blossomed between him and Carol after all these years was a beautiful, comfortable friendship.

Carol had invited him to come to Seattle. Perhaps she'd meant at a later date, but Edgar had jumped at the chance.

"Can I come next week?" he'd asked in a message, hoping that he wasn't being too forward. "I would get a hotel, of course, and there's no pressure. If we meet for dinner once and that's all that we're meant to have, I promise that will be enough for me," he'd said, meaning it. That one evening with Carol would be akin to the thrill one might feel at the chance to have a last, single evening with a departed loved one.

It was almost impossible to imagine her seeing his face after all these years and falling in love with him all over again—that would be too much to hope for. After all, middle age had settled in and Edgar knew he was possessed of thinning hair, a thickening waistline, and all the other hallmarks of years gone by. Maybe Carol would be changed as well, but in his eyes, she would always be the raven-haired, smooth-faced, gentle twenty-two-year-old he'd fallen in love with. There was no chance that he'd see her any other way.

Now, standing outside a sushi restaurant in the Queen Anne neighborhood of Seattle, Edgar held a yellow umbrella over his head and looked around with anticipation. Any time a woman approached, his eyes flickered to her face, hoping it was the face he'd carefully packed up and put away in the vault of his memory thirty years ago. But none of them were Carol.

There were women in sweatpants and rain boots. Women in dresses dotted with raindrops, hunkered beneath umbrellas as they rushed to their destinations. Young ladies in jeans with baseball caps, girls in skirts and tights. They had every shade of hair Edgar could imagine, and, to his surprise, most of them glanced his way and gave him an open, curious look. Many smiled. This almost never happened in New York City.

But still no Carol.

Until finally, at five minutes to six, a car pulled up and a woman climbed out from the back seat. She said something to the driver and then closed the door, turning to Edgar, and all at once, he knew it was her.

"Carol," he whispered, taking a step in her direction and holding out a hand to help her up onto the curb. An unnecessary, old-fashioned move, but Edgar came from a time when you treated a lady like a lady.

"Hi, Edgar," she said, smiling shyly. She took his hand and then they were on the sidewalk, looking at one another with giddy, barely restrained joy.

She'd hardly changed. Her dark hair was now cut in a sharp bob and had a single streak of white than ran from her side part and disappeared behind her ear. Her eyes were the same: dancing, alive, but now framed with the most delicate fan of lines. And her smile... Edgar's heart leapt in his chest and he moved the yellow umbrella over her head so that they were both covered.

"You look beautiful," he finally said, leaning down to kiss her on the cheek.

Carol pressed her cheek to his lips, closing her eyes. "And you haven't changed at all. I've missed you."

Edgar could have stayed like that forever, standing in the drizzling April evening on the streets of a city he'd never been to, so long as the woman who'd always had his heart would stay right there with him. But alas, that was completely impractical, so he offered her his arm and turned, opening the front door of the sushi restaurant.

"I've become a huge fan of the seafood on the west coast, and sushi is my favorite," Carol said, stepping out from under his umbrella and into the warm, noisy restaurant. "I hope you like it. I never even asked."

"I'm not picky. I'm totally happy to be here with you, and while I haven't tried sushi many times, I will eat anything you order."

Edgar folded his umbrella and hung it from a rack by the door next to a dozen others that were drip-drying onto a doormat that blended with the dark tiled floors.

They took a seat at the bar and suddenly the self-consciousness and nerves that Edgar hadn't allowed himself to feel on the flight kicked in. He watched the sushi chefs for a moment as they worked quickly, slicing, dicing, filleting, and preparing little works of art on tiny beds of rice.

"Amazing," Edgar said, picking up the glass of ice water set before him and taking a grateful sip. "I'm starving."

Carol laughed as she watched him. "You're still very handsome," she said, letting her eyes linger on his face as she held a menu in her hands. The younger version of Carol had been halting and hesitant in a charming, girlish way. This grown up Carol was still demure, but strong. Edgar could see the steel in her warm, glittery eyes.

"Thank you," he said, glancing down at his lap. Compliments from beautiful women weren't a frequent occurrence, and so his initial reaction was to verbally bat it away, but instead he sat quietly before turning to look at her. "I wish you'd never left," he blurted. "In thirty years, I've never met anyone else like you."

"Are you ready to order?" a young waitress with a piercing through her septum stood before them with a notepad in hand.

"We'll need just a moment, please," Carol said, smiling at her kindly. The waitress walked away.

"I've thought of you so many times," he went on. "But I assumed I'd never get this chance and I let myself accept that."

"And yet," Carol said, smiling as she tilted her head to one side, "here we are."

"Yes. Here we are." Edgar slipped his arms out of the tweed blazer he'd worn over a button-up shirt. Beneath that, he'd chosen his favorite, worn-in Superman t-shirt, which he hoped wasn't visible through the thin fabric of his cotton dress shirt. His face went red at the thought of Carol seeing it and thinking he was some sort of ridiculous, overgrown child.

"I've had a good life, Edgar, and I hope you have too," she said, shifting her body in her chair so that she was facing him and her knees were pressed against his outer thigh. "I had a happy marriage to a man who treated me with kindness until the day he died, and now I have three beautiful children and six grandchildren. I couldn't have asked for more." Carol put her small, soft hand on Edgar's arm. "How about you? What has your life been like?"

Edgar exhaled. "It's been interesting. I've lived in New York all these years, working in IT for various companies." He paused, weighing whether or not to tell her more. "And I love comics and superheroes. It's kind of a hobby, kind of a passion."

Carol smiled at him with amusement. "I remember how much you loved Superman," she said, taking her hand from his arm.

Sheepishly, Edgar looked down at the buttons of his shirt and then undid the top two to reveal the insignia on his chest.

A hand flew to Carol's mouth and a laugh escaped. "Oh!" she said, leaning forward in her chair so she could see it better. "Edgar, you're exactly the same."

He shrugged and re-buttoned his shirt. "In some ways yes, in some ways no. Like everyone." There was a moment of silence between them. "And I always seem to be in the right place at the right time to help someone when they need it. Which is weird. I guess it's the one thing that's been consistent all my life, and I've sort of built my self-identity around it." He picked up his water again and took another sip. "If I'm not going to be somebody's husband or father, at least I can be somebody's good luck charm. I can help them or save them when they need it."

Carol was looking at his face as he talked, genuine interest etched into the lines around her eyes and mouth. She tilted her head again in that soft way she had. "You might not believe this," she said, "but maybe the person you've been trying to save all along is *you*."

Edgar's head snapped up and he looked at her quizzically. "How so?"

"Helping people has given you a purpose. It means something. By saving others, you save yourself. It's very simple, really."

Edgar thought about this. "You know, I think you might be onto something," he admitted, pushing his glasses up his nose with his forefinger. "It makes me feel like I'm important in the grand scheme of the universe, and isn't that the thing we're all searching for when we choose careers, have children, volunteer, or try to find God?"

Carol nodded in agreement. "Yes, it is."

The waitress appeared again, looking at their intimate pose— Carol's knees still touching Edgar's thigh, her hand on his arm, his face bent forward in contemplation—and hesitated. "Should I give you more time?" she asked, taking a small step back.

Carol looked at the younger woman with a smile. "No," she said softly and with meaning that only Edgar could hear. "I think we've had all the time we need to decide."

As she picked up the menu and rattled off a list of sushi rolls they'd like to order, Edgar turned and admired her profile: softened, but still incredibly lovely. Familiar. Exciting. New, and yet not. Home.

Behind them, the rain fell from the gray evening sky and streamed down the windows as people, dogs, buses, cars, headlights, and bicycles passed by. The world went on as it always had, but inside the small sushi restaurant, a man who'd been determined to save everyone else sat next to the woman he'd always loved, convinced now that he'd finally saved himself.

Chapter 16

April 24

Amelia Island, FL

The afternoon was balmy and the heat had ratcheted up quickly, driving most of the locals to walk around in the morning and then to hover around an AC unit until the sun sank lower in the sky. Lucy was at her desk at The Holiday Adventure Club, fielding calls and firing off emails. She had approximately four and a half days until she left for Morocco, and there was plenty to do around Amelia Island before she left it behind again for a place so exotic (in her mind) that she'd never even considered going there.

As she sat for a moment with a pencil in hand and Prince playing on her computer speakers, Lucy pondered the year so far: meeting Carmen and Bree on the trip to Venice; accidentally fake-marrying the handsome young fireman, Finn Barlow, on the trip to St. Barts, which was where she and Nick finally moved their very real relationship forward in a big way; the recent adventures in Edinburgh, which she'd found she was far more invested in than she'd realized.

After getting home, she'd immediately shot off an email to Edgar to see how things were going and had been infinitely pleased to hear that he was flying straight to Seattle to meet up with Carol after all these years. When she'd cooked up the idea for a travel agency and dreamed of an around the world adventure like this one, it had never occurred to her that she'd actually end up posing as a de facto match-maker, teenage girl wrangler, and marriage counselor.

To that end, she'd texted back and forth with Olive already upon her return, and things sounded great out in San Diego. There'd been talk of a family reunion and of resolving some questions and old secrets, but most importantly, Olive had assured Lucy that Dane was about ninety-five percent his old self, and that she'd never felt happier or more optimistic about what was ahead of them. She felt grateful to Lucy for intervening the day she'd nearly fled Edinburgh in frustra-tion, and she'd added Lucy on Facebook so that they could stay updated on one another. These were the kinds of connections Lucy had never even dreamed of and couldn't have anticipated, but they were making these journeys so much more enjoyable for her than they might've been otherwise.

As for the three girls—Snow, Vanderbilt, and Filene—they'd gotten home safely and started a group chat with Lucy to thank her for keeping an eye on them, and for not alerting their parents to their poor choices while abroad. Lucy still felt a small nagging in her heart that she should have called home on the girls, but in the end, finding them had been top priority, not terrifying their parents as they waited, thousands of miles away, to hear that their daughters were safe.

So, in Lucy's book, it had been another successful trip with all good outcomes, and she was completely ready to get this next trip underway and to meet her new guests.

Lucy leaned back in her desk chair and faced the window, watching as two older, white-haired women walked by, heading either to Honey's for manicures, or to The Carrier Pigeon, as those were the last two shops on that end of the strip mall. She spaced out a little as she thought of the list of names on her travel list for Morocco and pondered the amount of packing she had to do, and as she did, a tiny headache started to pulse behind her left eye. Lucy grabbed her phone and her office keys, locking the glass door behind her as she stepped out and went next door to Beans & Sand for an afternoon coffee.

"Oh, the world traveler visits my humble place of business," Dev Lopez said, looking up from the sink as he rinsed the parts of his espresso machine. "How goes it, Miss Adventure?"

"It goes," Lucy said. The door closed behind her, its familiar bell tinkling as it shut.

There were people scattered around the diner-like coffee shop, sitting in vinyl booths beneath posters of all of Dev's favorite musicians and bands. Shelly Maxwell, who lived on Lucy's street, was seated under a poster of Nirvana's *Unplugged* session, sipping from a cup of coffee as she listened intently to a woman who had a bible open on the table between them. Shelly made eye contact with Lucy and smiled.

"What can I get for our intrepid explorer today?" Dev put the espresso machine back together, his muscles tensing beneath his smooth, brown skin as he cranked a handle and twisted a piece into place.

"A cold brew with coconut milk, please," Lucy said, leaning one hip against the front counter. "And how are you?"

Dev got to work on her drink immediately, not stopping as he talked. "I'm doing fine. Great. Business is good, the weather is hot, the tourists are dwindling."

"But fewer tourists means fewer people straggling in to spend money," Lucy pointed out.

"True, but fewer tourists also means more parking spots at the beach, and less chance I'll get hit by a grandpa from Ohio while I'm riding my Triumph and minding my own business."

Lucy nodded. She'd seen him sitting astride his motorcycle in their parking lot on many occasions, black helmet fitted over his head, jetting out into traffic and melting into the glut of cars on the highway. And, to be honest, Lucy had seen the wreckage of enough car vs. motorcycle interactions to know that it usually didn't end well.

She'd watched him ride off once or twice and worried, but then chalked his safety up to fate, chance, and skill on the bike. Who knew what universal force decided the outcome of daily activities and split-second decisions? But she definitely agreed with him that he was better off during the slow season.

"So, what have you been up to lately? I feel like I've been gone so much that I'm missing everything around here."

"You are," Dev confirmed, pouring her coffee into a clear plastic cup and topping it off with an inch of coconut milk, just like she liked it. "I got married last week and we have three kids."

"Oh jeez," Lucy said, laughing as he snapped a plastic lid onto her coffee cup.

"Seriously. In fact, we're already talking divorce."

"Dev!" She reached for the iced coffee and pulled a straw from the cup where Dev stored them on the counter.

He lifted a shoulder and let it fall, glancing around the coffee shop. For the moment, everyone seemed to be fully caffeinated and not in need of anything, so he leaned forward, resting both elbows on the counter as he looked at Lucy.

"I kid, of course. But you have been gone a lot. How does it feel?" Dev asked.

Lucy took her first long pull of cold coffee, feeling it course through her. It brought an instant hit of caffeine. "It feels..." She narrowed her eyes and looked at the ceiling for a second. "Like I'm messing with my internal clock by visiting different time zones so quickly. And like I'm probably neglecting a lot of things that I *should* be paying more attention to."

"Like Nick?" He pushed himself up off his elbows and turned his back on Lucy, picking up a damp rag so he could wipe down the counter as they talked.

Lucy choked a little. "I was thinking more specifically of my mom and her needs for more care up in Buffalo, but I mean...I guess Nick too. And my cat. Poor Joji isn't even sure I'm his mom anymore."

"The cat will live," Dev said gruffly. "And Nick will get by. He comes here for coffee all the time and I can promise you, he's eating and sleeping. Probably missing you a lot, but then who wouldn't?"

Lucy blinked a few times and pulled her straw halfway out of the lid before pushing it back in and stirring the coffee and coconut milk. The whole thing was a noisy affair: squeaks of plastic on plastic and the sound of ice being rattled in the cup. But it gave her a moment to gather her thoughts and to let Dev gather his. Surely he couldn't have meant to sound as wistful as he had when he'd said that last bit.

"You're kind of a fixture around the old strip mall," Dev said, tossing the damp rag in the general direction of his sink and then leaning back against a cabinet, folding his arms across his chest. "It's never the same without you, Miss Adventure."

Lucy rolled her eyes dramatically as she put the straw to her lips. "I'm sure. Or maybe it's just that I'm your most frequent customer and you're afraid you won't be able to keep the lights on without me."

Dev smiled wryly. "That too."

Lucy was about to pull a twenty out of her wallet, pay, and go, when Dev stood upright again and moved around from behind the counter so that he was standing next to her.

"When are you leaving again?"

"Sunday," Lucy said, her eyebrows lifting slightly.

"Mmm. Okay." A small frown creased Dev's forehead beneath his mop of chocolate curls.

"Why?"

Lucy was mildly irritated to find her heart racing. Dev was *not* her boyfriend—not that Nick was exactly her boyfriend either!—but he was not the man she was currently seeing, and therefore neither his proximity nor his bedroom eyes should be making her feel fluttery. His question should not be filling her chest with anticipatory butterflies. She took a small step away from him, holding her coffee in front of her with both hands like it was an armor or a shield that could protect her from his powerful attractiveness and smoldering good looks.

"I had something I wanted to show you, but you can only see it on

Saturday night. Do you think your man might uncuff you for an evening, or would that be too weird?"

Lucy's stomach roiled at the way he said "uncuff"—she was not the possession of any man, nor was she accustomed to having to ask permission to do the things she wanted to do. Her hackles went up immediately.

With a toss of her long, loose hair and the slightest upward tilt of her chin, Lucy looked him squarely in the eye. "First of all, I don't need to ask Nick for his permission. Secondly, I don't know that just 'wanting to show me something' is enough of a description to get me to go somewhere with you. Ryan Ingersoll said the same thing to Penny Nuñoz in high school, and after he 'showed her something,' she showed up at school pregnant. So I'll need more detail."

Dev chuckled and his dark eyes glittered. "I'm not offering to get you pregnant, Miss Adventure. There's just a meteor shower I thought you might want to see." He held his arms out to his sides. "Look, I'll even keep my hands like this all evening so that you don't think I'm trying to pull a—what was his name? Ryan something?"

"Ingersoll," Lucy said, feeling her cheeks flame. It was mortifying, the fact that she'd told a story about two high school classmates getting pregnant like it was the most scandalous thing that had ever happened in the universe.

"Right. Well, my intentions are pure. Plus I like your company." Dev let his hands drop to his sides. "And I'm curious to hear how things are going in the travel industry. I've been reading a book about marketing for my own little shop here," he looked around Beans & Sand, nodding at the walls and the front door, "and I thought maybe I could tell you a few of the highlights. See if they might help you as well."

Lucy thought about this. Dev *had* been incredibly helpful and interested in her trips and in drumming up interest in the tours, and she knew that he had a good mind for business. But would this sound as innocent if she were to tell Nick about it? If she said, "Hey, I know you're flying up to Buffalo to help my mother and my elderly aunt so that I can pack and get ready to fly to Africa, but I'm going to be out stargazing with a guy you kind of hate?"

Her stomach pretzeled; of course she knew the answer to her own question. And yet, as Dev watched her face, she broke into a grin. "I'd love to," she said, holding out a hand like they were making a deal.

Dev smirked, looking slightly puzzled at the offer of a handshake, but he took it, squeezing her fingers in his warm hand. "Then Saturday night it is," he said, letting go and walking behind the counter.

Lucy got all the way back to her office before she realized that she'd never even bothered to pay for her coffee.

That evening, Lucy was on the lanai that jutted out from behind her little bungalow, listening to the cicadas and the sound of her next door neighbor's sprinkler. She had a glass of iced tea in one hand, its condensation dripping onto her bare thigh. There was an unopened book in her lap. On the table next to her, her phone buzzed.

The latest, please? It was a message from Carmen in the group chat that had been going on between Carmen and Bree and Lucy since the trip to Venice.

Honestly, Bree said. *I need updates.*

With a smile, Lucy set her iced tea on the table, dried her hands on her shorts, and got ready to type a response.

I'm getting ready to leave for Morocco on Sunday, she said. *Edinburgh was crazy, and I totally forgot to update you guys, so I'm sorry for that! After the night I texted you about how we'd found the missing girls with a bunch of bikers, they were on their best behavior. Crisis averted. And that superhero guy, Edgar, found the girl he was in love with thirty years ago!!! They were supposed to meet in Seattle this week. Also, the married couple on the trip managed to pull through, so that's good news.*

Lucy sent the message that was already getting rather long and then took a sip of her iced tea.

Annndddd, Carmen said, *what about you and the mailman?*

Nick is good, and technically he just runs the postal shop—he's not ACTUALLY a mailman. Lucy chuckled and waited for a response.

But does he wear cute little shorts with a shirt tucked in? Bree chimed in. She'd gotten much feistier in the short time since Lucy had met her, and it was easy to see how Venice had provided her with some sort of closure—maybe a sense of peace—that had allowed her to relax and be herself again following the death of her husband.

Alas, no, Lucy typed, laughing out loud. *He doesn't dress like a mailman at all. Want me to send a pic?*

OHMYGODYESIMMEDIATELY!!! Carmen responded.

Lucy scrolled through her photo album and chose one she'd taken of Nick and Hemingway on the beach. The sun was low in the sky, and everything had that golden evening haze. Nick wore a loose chambray shirt with the top few buttons opened, and one hand rested casually in the pocket of his shorts. Hemingway sat on his back legs next to his master, head cocked to one side as they both posed for Lucy's photo. She sent it to Carmen and Bree and the response was instantaneous.

Yesssssss, girl, was Carmen's decree, and *Wow, Lucy—he's soooo cute!* came from Bree. She smiled.

He's wonderful, Lucy said, *and he's going up to Buffalo for me on Friday to check on my mom's situation so that I can get ready for Morocco.* Just committing the words to writing gave her a rush of guilt over accepting Dev's offer to see a cosmic event on Saturday evening. She'd been trying to squelch the voice in her head all afternoon, the one telling her that she was being crazy to jeopardize things with Nick in any way. But the opposing voice—kind of like a devil and an angel battling it out right there inside her brain—was there to remind her that trusting anyone completely was a risky gamble. After all, there'd been Jason. And Charlie. And her own father wasn't a great example of a man who'd stuck around and honored his responsibilities and commitments either.

You're living the dream, girl, Carmen said. *And Bree and I are just here on a rainy Wednesday evening, having a beer at a pub in downtown Portland.*

Wait! You guys are out together right now, but messaging me? Lucy hadn't realized that. *Go—enjoy your drink there! I'll keep you updated on everything.*

Send pics of Morocco! Bree said.

Lucy responded with a string of emoji, including a thumbs-up, a smiley face, and three different colored hearts. She set her phone down and picked up the iced tea, leaning her head back against the cushion of her chair.

The fact that she couldn't even bring herself to use her new friends as advisors on the issue of going out with Dev without telling Nick told her all that she needed to know: it was the wrong thing to do. But his attitude had really pushed her buttons, and she knew that by *not* going, she was sending a message to the universe (and to herself) that she was ready to make a full-blown commitment to Nick. And was she? Was *he* ready for that? It was a lot of responsibility to take on a committed relationship, and neither of them had even come close to talking about things like that.

Lucy sipped her watered down iced tea and watched as a gecko crawled across the screen of her lanai, its legs and tail skittering as it rushed to destinations unknown. The water next door stopped as her seventy-year-old neighbor, Earlene, muttered to herself in the twilight, dragging the sprinkler head loudly across the grass. For a moment, she wished she had someone like Earlene, a mother of a certain age with her wits about her, to talk to. Someone older and wiser who could pass down life advice and not just bring her more stress.

But she didn't and so she'd manage things without advice, and she'd do what felt right. That was all a person really could do anyway.

Chapter 17

April 27

Amelia Island, FL

"Things are good. Today we got a lot accomplished, I think." Nick was FaceTiming Lucy from her mom's house in Buffalo, standing on the tiny cement porch off the kitchen at the back of the house. Behind him, Lucy could see the familiar dark blue siding of the house, along with the giant picture window that looked into the dining room.

"I can't thank you enough, Nick. You have no idea." Lucy stood in her own kitchen, back leaning against the counter, phone propped against a bowl of shiny red apples on the wood block island in the center of the room.

"I really don't mind," he said, holding out the phone so that she had a view of his upper torso, arms tanned and strong under the white t-shirt he wore. His hair was mussed and he had about two days of stubble on his handsome face. "Your mom is a real character."

Lucy snorted. "Don't I know it." And she did. Yvette Landish was truly something else: her agoraphobia had so colored who she was as a person during Lucy's youth that it was hard now to imagine her as anything but a colorful, eccentric shut-in. She frequently refused to brush her long, gray hair; more often than not she wore caftans around the house with knee-high socks and men's slippers; and in recent years, she'd taken to opening her window and shouting obscenities as the school children disembarked from the bus on her street in the afternoons. Of course it had been alarming and out of character the first few times Lucy had heard about her yelling swear words at kids, but once Yvette had been properly diagnosed with dementia on top of her agoraphobia, it all made more sense.

"Do you want to know what she said to the guy who came to install the fence?" Nick's face was both amused and somewhat disbelieving.

"Oh god. Probably not." Lucy laughed. "But tell me anyway."

"You know what? I'm going to spare you," he said. "But just know that it had something to do with him keeping the code to the keypad so he could come back later on and 'visit' her."

Lucy's face blanched. "You're kidding."

"Nope."

"Put my aunt Sharon on. We need to up my mother's medication."

Nick howled with laughter. "The guy was tickled pink. Trust me."

"Has she hit on you yet?" Lucy put one hand over her eyes, like shielding herself from view would somehow make her invisible.

"No," Nick said, frowning. "She seems to think I'm her son."

Lucy pulled her hand away from her eyes. "She doesn't have a son."

"Sharon tried to tell her that a few times, but she won't let go of the idea, so we're just bobbing along like boats on the water, seeing where the wind takes us. And for the record, I've been called far worse than someone's son, so I'm not terribly offended."

"Although that would make us siblings," Lucy pointed out.

"True. And that's a bit creepy." Nick glanced around the yard. "So what are you up to? Packing still?"

Lucy turned her phone to the front room where she had her

rolling suitcase packed and standing on end, handle pulled up, and a full carry-on next to it. "I'm all set," she said.

"Got your passport, your magazines, your candy, and your picture of me to stare at in case you hit turbulence?" Nick joked.

"I have my passport, a few magazines, lots of M&Ms, and actually, it's a picture of Keanu Reeves. But otherwise you got it all right."

"Ouch." Nick laughed. "So tonight, make sure you get lots of sleep and don't worry about a thing. You're going to have a great trip, and I can't wait to hear all about it."

Behind Nick, the sliding door to the kitchen opened and Aunt Sharon appeared. "Oh, sorry, honey," she said to Nick, stepping back inside. "Didn't realize you were doing one of those picture calls."

"Aunt Sharon!" Lucy called out. Nick held out the phone so Sharon could see her niece's face and she leaned in close, squinting at Lucy.

"Oh, gawd! Lucy, it's you. I didn't know that." Her aunt Sharon wore a tank top with blue flowers and a headband that pushed her permed, graying hair back from her face. It frizzed around her like a halo.

"How are you? How is Mom?"

"Well," Sharon said, stepping out and closing the door behind her. Next to Sharon and Nick was an old fashioned, round, domed barbecue that hadn't been used in years, and beyond that, a flowerbed that had mostly gone to seed. "Your mom is okay. It's hit or miss, you know? The caregivers we've hired have been extremely professional, and this fence is going to help a lot. Nick's been a doll," she said, looking at Nick adoringly.

"He's wonderful," Lucy agreed. "I appreciate him making the trip so much. And if there's anything else you can think of that will help, please feel free to make a list or talk to Nick about it, and I can work on getting things set up while I'm in Morocco."

"Oh, gawd. Lucy, sweetheart," Sharon said, waving a hand. As she did, her upper arm jiggled loosely. "You're going to *Africa*."

"Yes, ma'am," Lucy said, falling back on the manners she'd learned as a child. "I am."

"Then don't you worry about us. I'll only call you in case of a real emergency, you hear? Nick's given me his number, so if anything small happens while you're gone, I'll just bug him."

Aunt Sharon glanced at Nick again, off-screen, and shot him a winning, flirtatious smile. "He's such a doll," she said again.

Lucy almost teased her aunt about having a crush on Nick, but then thought better of it. Aunt Sharon had been a widow since her early forties, and Lucy was more than fine with her having a harmless crush on Nick. Let the older woman look as much as she wanted—she'd seen him in action with the much older patrons who frequented The Carrier Pigeon, and Lucy knew that Nick could handle the flirting.

"Well, thanks to both of you for *everything*," Lucy stressed, scratching her upper arm with her fingernails and dreading the fact that she was about to sign off with Nick without telling him that she'd be out with Dev that night. "I'm going to eat some dinner here and try to get to bed early, if possible. My flight's at six o'clock tomorrow morning, so I'm up at three."

"Okay, love!" Aunt Sharon waved at her, her ample upper arms swaying wildly again. "Have a safe trip!" She patted Nick's shoulder and then opened the sliding door, disappearing inside again so that Lucy and Nick could say their goodbyes in private.

"Listen," Nick said, lowering his voice. "All is truly well here. I think Sharon is feeling more secure with the fence in place, and we interviewed a housekeeper to come in once a week and keep up on the bathrooms and vacuuming, specifically. Sharon's got the laundry and kitchen under control, so I think this will take a little weight off her shoulders."

Lucy's heart wrenched in her chest; what a man Nick was. What a *catch*. She was an idiot for even considering doing anything except for eating a quick, hastily made quesadilla and climbing into bed before nine o'clock to get some sleep before her early flight. Her eyes filled with tears.

"Nick..." she said, trailing off.

"Hey," he said softly, looking worried. "Everything is cool. I'll talk to you when you get to Morocco, alright? What's the time difference?"

"I'll be five hours ahead." Lucy sniffed, swiping at her eyes. "So basically like here to London."

"Got it. That's totally doable. Call me anytime, okay? I'll have my ringer on, day or night."

"I will," she whispered. She couldn't find the words she wanted at that moment to tell Nick how grateful she was, or how much she'd miss him. Nothing was coming to her. All she knew was that she was about to hang up the phone and call Dev to cancel. That was it. No chance in hell was she going to screw this up. "I'll call you."

Nick smiled. "Okay. Safe travels, girl."

"You too," Lucy said. "Tell my mom hi."

"Gotcha." Nick winked at her and gave a little wave. "Goodnight."

"Night, Nick," she said, waving back at him before ending the call. Lucy pulled up Dev's contact and was about to punch the button to call him when someone knocked on her front door. She set the phone on the island, wiped her eyes again, and walked down the hallway.

She pulled open the door to find Dev standing there, wearing leather chaps over his jeans and a thin black leather jacket over a gray Smiths t-shirt. "Ready?" he asked, looking her up and down. She was still in the 501s and pink tank top she'd worn all afternoon as she packed her bags. Lucy followed his gaze down to her bare feet.

"Dev," she said, still holding onto the doorknob. "I—"

But he didn't wait for whatever she was about to say. Instead, he walked into the house, opened the hall closet, and pulled out a brown leather jacket—one she'd brought from Buffalo but never had the occasion to wear.

"This will work." Dev tossed it in her direction and looked at her feet, cocking an eyebrow as he took in the sparkly gold polish on her toes. He put his hands on his hips, his leather jacket making a crinkling sound as he did. "Honey's work?" He nodded at her feet, looking up with just his eyes.

Lucy wiggled her bare toes. "Of course," she said. "What shoes should I wear?"

"Nice. And boots," Dev said definitively. "I'll be on my bike." With that, he walked back out the front door, leaving Lucy standing there with her coat in her hands.

Her resolve to cancel on him had flown away like a flock of birds scattering to the wind.

She needed boots.

Five minutes later, she was on the back of Dev's Triumph with a black skull helmet that matched his fastened under her chin.

"Hold on," he said, revving the bike. Lucy wrapped her arms around his waist and pressed her face to his leather-clad back. Dev roared off down the street and Lucy's stomach lurched at the sudden movement.

She gave a little yelp and closed her eyes as the salty evening air whipped through her loose hair and brushed against her cheeks.

Help me, help me, help me, she said silently, sending out a little prayer as they accelerated and merged onto the highway. As the heady combination of the ocean, gasoline, and leather filled Lucy's nostrils, she knew that the prayer wasn't for her safety on the bike.

It wasn't for that at all.

* * *

They pulled off at a beach parking lot about twenty miles north of Amelia Island and Lucy stepped off the back of the motorcycle, her legs shaking.

"Whoa," she laughed, unbuckling her helmet and handing it to

Dev. Her cheeks felt raw and her eyes felt wild. "I've never been on a bike like that before."

Dev pulled his helmet off in one quick motion and secured both of their headpieces to the bike before offering Lucy his hand.

"I'm not getting fresh," he promised, still holding out a hand as she stared at him. "You just look a little unsteady on your feet."

Lucy couldn't deny that, so she took the offered hand and followed him across the sand dunes and down to the beach. Just beyond where it was visible from the parking lot, people had spread blankets and brought coolers and were scattered across the sand. The sun was so close to dipping below the horizon that it looked like a room full of people around her were waiting for the lights to be turned off.

And then, just like that, someone hit the switch and the cobalt sky turned indigo. Dev tugged her hand as they came to a spot on the sand where they were at least twenty feet from anyone else.

"How about here?" he said, taking off his chaps and folding them carefully before setting them down on the sand. "Sorry, I don't have a lot of room on my bike for storage, so I don't have a blanket or anything."

Lucy sank down and got comfortable. "No worries. This is perfect." Truth be told, she probably would have been somewhat put off if he'd gone the extra mile and brought any sort of picnic or blanket. This wasn't a date, after all, and there was no need to make it into something more than two friends watching the stars together.

In the dark.

On the beach.

With the waves crashing near them.

After having their bodies locked together tightly, Dev's body between Lucy's legs for more than twenty minutes.

She swallowed hard and looked up at the sky.

"This is beautiful," she said, feeling her quivering legs start to relax. It wasn't that he'd been a terrifying driver, but she'd truly never ridden a motorcycle that fast before. Once, as a teenager, a cousin had taken her on the back of his dirt bike around the bumpy fields of their grandparents' farm in upstate New York, but that hardly counted. This had really and truly been what people must feel on a motorcycle, that thing that draws them to it over and over: a delicious sense of fear mixed with freedom. Contrary to what she might have imagined beforehand, Lucy had loved it.

"In a minute here, the show will really start," Dev said, leaning back on his elbows and stretching his legs out in front of him. He crossed his ankles, one boot over the other as he craned his neck toward the sky.

Lucy laid flat on the sand, lacing her fingers behind her head. She was working hard not to count the hours between that precise moment and the time her alarm would ring to wake her for her trip to the airport. She'd have to get some sleep on the plane.

"Oooohhh!" A collective gasp went through the people all around them as the first meteor streaked across the sky.

"Cool," Dev said quietly, his warm amber eyes trained on the heavens above. Lucy couldn't help it: she turned her head to look at his handsome profile.

Dev, Dev, Dev, she thought. *Deven Lopez.* Did his name arouse any feelings in her? Did watching his face make her toes tingle the way they had on the back of his motorcycle, racing down the highway? She tried to push away the feelings of disloyalty toward Nick as she pondered Dev, trying desperately to rule him out entirely as anything other than a person who occupied a corner of her day. A very *important* corner, as she loved her coffee passionately, but still—was he nothing more than the mysterious guy who caffeinated her on work days?

As she was thinking, Dev turned his head to look at her. Suddenly, their noses and lips were just inches apart. Rather than flinch, Dev smiled. "Oh, hey," he said.

Lucy took a deep breath and slowly turned her head to look up at the stars, as if she hadn't just been caught staring at him.

"Another!" Lucy said. Her arm thrust into the air as she pointed at a brightly streaking meteor. "Oh! Two more!"

Again, the crowd around them gasped and some people even clapped while three or four more meteors burned their way across the galaxy, leaving shimmering trails in their wake. For a few minutes after, nothing happened. A hush fell over the beach.

"So," Dev said in the pocket of silence. "Things with you and Nick are going strong." It wasn't a question, but more of a statement.

"Yes," Lucy agreed, not offering more.

"Did he mind that you were coming here with me tonight?"

It was a bonus that they were both looking up at the night sky instead of at each other, because Lucy felt herself wince visibly. "I didn't tell him. And I would appreciate it if you didn't either."

Dev took a long, audible breath in through his nose, then released it through his mouth before speaking. "Okay," he finally said. "If that's what you want."

"It is." Lucy could hear the clipped tone in her own words, and knew that she really should be offering more of an explanation for her actions.

"Listen, I told you at the concert that I wasn't into chasing after some other guy's girl—"

"And yet here we are," Lucy interrupted. She sat up abruptly. "You invited me here tonight and even goaded me into coming, though of course I am a grown woman and ultimately the choice was mine."

"Are you saying I'm trying to poach Nick's lady?"

"I'm saying I'm not entirely sure what you're doing. Hell," Lucy said, pulling her legs into a sitting position and making herself fully upright, "I'm not even sure what I'm doing. Am I panicking because Nick and I are getting too close and I've got some trust issues? Did I come here tonight because it felt like a dare? Am I having some sort of pre-midlife crisis because I'm watching my mom wither away?" She spread her palms wide, turning them toward the sky. "I have no idea. I like you, Dev. You're interesting, and obviously you're attractive."

"Oh, obviously," he said sarcastically, as if he had no idea that, at all times, he was essentially testosterone walking around in paper-thin denim and a t-shirt that could barely hold in his abs and delts.

Lucy put her head in her hands and leaned forward, closing her eyes. "But I really like Nick. He's a good guy. He's wonderful, actually."

"If you're into the all-American type. Floppy hair, good at throwing a football, earnest. The kind who goes over big with mothers."

Lucy winced again. *Mothers.* Nick was up in Buffalo, taking care of her mother. *What the hell are you DOING?!* a voice inside her head screamed. She stood up, brushing the sand off the back of her jeans.

"I'm so sorry, Dev. I have to go. I shouldn't have come at all."

Overhead, a burst of meteor activity caused everyone on the beach to shout and point their phones and video cameras toward the sky. It felt like being in the middle of a fireworks display at a Fourth of July picnic.

Dev had rolled onto one side, leaning on his right elbow as he looked up at her. "You want to go now?"

"Yes," Lucy said firmly. "Again, I'm sorry. I shouldn't have come." Behind her, the ocean crashed onto the shore before rolling right back out.

"Okay," Dev said, pushing himself up to a standing position. "I'll take you."

"I can Uber," Lucy protested. "This is my fault anyway, so don't leave."

"Lucy, come on." Dev looked at her pleadingly. Normally his eyes held a challenge, an invitation, a spark of something mischievous, but now he just looked remorseful. "I shouldn't have pushed you to come if you didn't feel like it was the right thing to do. That's my fault. Let me take you home."

A cheer went up all around them and they both tipped their heads back to look at the spray of meteors that fell in all directions.

Lucy turned her head back to Dev. "Okay," she said, feeling stupid and regretful.

To her surprise, Dev didn't walk ahead of her angrily or like she'd offended him, which she felt she must have. Instead he walked next to her, one hand placed lightly on the small of her back as they traipsed through the sand dunes and walked around people and blankets. Overhead, the sky continued to wow the crowd.

The ride back to Amelia Island felt longer than the ride they'd taken to get to the beach, and Lucy refrained from resting her cheek against Dev's back. At her curb, he stopped the bike and let it idle so she could climb off. She handed him back his helmet.

"Dev," she said, hoping for a chance to say the things that had been going through her mind as they sped down the highway under the cloak of night.

"Hey. It's cool, Miss Adventure." Dev revved the engine. "Don't give it another thought."

He pulled away and drove down her street, leaning into the curve and making a right turn that took him out of view. Lucy stood at the end of her driveway for a few seconds, feeling angry at herself, confused about her own actions, and disappointed that she'd made things awkward with Dev.

Finally, kicking at a loose rock with the toe of her boot, Lucy turned and went inside. Three o'clock would come far faster than she wanted it to.

Chapter 18

April 28

Miami, FL

After a six a.m. flight from Jacksonville to Miami and then a delayed flight out of MIA, Lucy found herself with nearly eight hours to cool her heels. Since her bags were already checked, she decided that rather than sitting around the airport on a spring day, she'd get out and see the city.

It was a quick Uber ride through the quiet of an early Sunday morning to get to South Beach, where Lucy asked the driver to drop her at a Starbucks on the corner of 14th and Ocean. Inside, she waited in the relatively short line behind well-groomed older couples, men in business suits—strange, for a Sunday—and the kind of beautiful people who were still attracted to what was once one of the fashion modeling meccas of the world.

As she waited in line to order a vanilla latte, Lucy looked out the window at the soft sun rising over the pale sandy beach and remembered her high school friend Mallory, a tall, willowy redhead with perfect proportions and an uncanny ability to look directly into any camera that happened to be pointed her direction. Mallory had been scouted at a shopping mall one time when she and Lucy were awkward fourteen-year-olds, walking along and sipping milkshakes while they talked about boys. They'd giggled after the woman who'd approached them had given Mallory her business card and implored her to have her parents call, but it wasn't even two years later that Mallory had left school to model full-time, living here on South Beach and appearing in magazines and advertisements for everything from high fashion, to cruise ship vacations, to face soap.

Of course they were Facebook friends now like everyone else on planet Earth, and Lucy was about to pull out her phone and look Mallory up out of curiosity when the man in front of her stepped aside, leaving the barista looking at her expectantly.

"Good morning. Venti sugar free vanilla latte and a blueberry scone, please," Lucy said, already pulling out her wallet to pay and move out of the way. She knew from experience that there was nothing people liked less in a big city than someone who appeared to be a slow, bumbling tourist.

With her drink and scone in hand, she walked out onto the narrow patio that ran around the coffee shop, choosing a table for two with a view of the sand and the sidewalk so that she could people-watch.

She looked at her phone as she broke off a chunk of scone: still only seven-thirty in the morning. Too early to call Nick and wake him up—the man deserved his sleep after traveling all the way to New York and spending his weekend with two old women.

Leaning back in the chair, Lucy took a sip of her coffee and watched as a seagull picked through the sand for anything edible. On the sidewalk, an elderly man with a cane stopped walking and pulled a baggie from the pocket of his windbreaker, then tossed a handful of crumbs at the seagull. Suddenly a flock of the birds descended, bumping into one another as they fought for the scraps of food. Lucy smiled at the look of joy on the man's face. A groan came from the table next to hers.

"Freaking old people," a girl who looked to be about eighteen and who was clearly a model said to her companion—a man with an expensive camera that he was intent on messing with. "Like we need the fish birds over here bugging us for our food."

The man chuffed, an amused grin pulling at his stubbled face. "The fish birds?"

"Yeah," the girl said, taking a sip of her small coffee. "You know, the white birds that always dive for fish."

The man looked up from his camera and shook his head, smiling at her fondly. "Seagulls, Daria. They're seagulls."

Daria shrugged a bony shoulder and rolled her eyes. "Who cares. Seagulls, fish birds, whatever."

Lucy listened to the exchange, trying to remember if she'd ever been young and beautiful enough that her naïveté had been charming. Maybe all eighteen-year-olds were like Daria, dipped in gold and glistening with promise, regardless of how silly or frothy they might seem. She did remember that: the feeling of having the whole world at her feet, the idea that somewhere out there in this great big world was her destiny and that she'd find it, no problem, because duh, that's how life worked.

She sighed now and took another sip of coffee. The old man with the cane had wandered on, and the seagulls had dispersed. Lucy picked up her phone and opened her email as the sun rose even higher, filtering its rays through the palm trees that ran along Ocean Drive and making the sand sparkle like it was flecked with glitter.

Email: *junk, stuff to deal with later, message from her mortgage company, update to travel list.* Lucy flipped through the emails, sorting, deleting, and finally clicking on the updated travel list, which would be the manifest of people who were joining her in Morocco.

At the next table, Daria and the photographer stood, tossed their empty cups into a trash can, and took the stairs down onto the beach where he promptly dropped to his knees in the sand and started clicking away with his camera, catching Daria in his lens as she walked toward a palm tree, stopped, and posed. Once again, Lucy thought of Mallory as a teen model and wondered whether she'd done this same thing here on South Beach, showing off her gorgeous, youthful figure for the cameras of men who simply wanted to capture and sell her image. But then she refocused on her email and pushed her old friend from her mind.

Lucy lifted her coffee to her lips again as the email loaded.

"What in the hell..." she muttered, nearly spitting out her latte as she read through the words that appeared on the screen.

The service she used to send her an alert any time there were changes to the group dynamic had pushed a message through that left her breathless. Her heart pounded, and she blinked in disbelief.

"No," she whispered, putting a hand to her chest as she read and re-read the words. "No."

Updated travel list, April 28:

Traveler has changed name from Joseph Logan. New name: Jason Landish, age 38. Traveling from: JFK, NYC. Arriving Marrakech April 30.

Lucy skimmed the email, still incredulous. Jason Landish. Jason Landish had registered for her trip to Morocco under the name Joseph Logan. Jason would be joining her in Morocco.

My ex-husband will be flying to Africa, joining my tour group, and haunting me halfway around the world. What the hell is he thinking? Why would he even consider doing this? Lucy's mind whirred like a computer booting up for the day. Thoughts raced around, sending pings of shock throughout her body. Jason had signed up for the trip under an assumed identity. Good lord...

She sat back in her chair again, eyes fixed on a spot in the distance. This changed everything.

* * *

The airplane was only about half full and Lucy had a row all to herself. She sat in the sleek leather business class seat, watching as flight attendants in crisp uniforms with perfectly manicured nails and hair bustled about efficiently, offering blankets, pillows, headphones, snacks, and drinks to the other passengers in Lucy's compartment.

After the shock of seeing Jason's name on her travel list, she'd spent her remaining time on South Beach walking around in a daze, ultimately settling for a spot on a bench that faced the ocean so that she could soak up the sun and watch mothers pushing babies in strollers; glistening, muscled men playing volleyball in the sand; and older couples ambling along, hand-in-hand as they passed the time.

She'd spent those hours thinking about her marriage, her divorce, and everything that had happened since, and had come away wondering if there was really anything left to say to Jason. Given the opportunity to unburden herself to him, would she even bother? Of course at first it had seemed like that would be the best way to deal with his blistering infidelity and the pain he'd caused her, but as time had gone on, yelling and accusing and pointing fingers seemed utterly ridiculous. The pain would always be there—of failure, of lost love, and certainly of finding out that her husband had gotten another (much younger) woman pregnant as she herself struggled with infertility—but did the desire to hash things out and find closure still burn inside of Lucy? Not really.

She buckled her seatbelt and reached for the magazine in the pocket of the seat in front of her. Flipping through the pages without really seeing anything, Lucy tried to suck in calming breaths, and to keep herself from edging toward the panic she'd felt there at Starbucks reading the emailed passenger update. Her first inclination had been to text Jason or call him and ask what was going on, but something had stopped her. Could she even convince him not to come at this late hour? Would it make her feel better as she headed into another big trip to unsheathe the anger that had, over the past year or so, finally cooled down to an occasional simmer?

She shoved the magazine back into the pocket of the seat and leaned her head back, closing her eyes.

"This is Captain Merrit," a gruff but friendly voice said over the intercom system. "We'll be taxiing here shortly after we get final clearance for takeoff from air traffic control. We hope you have a relaxed and easy flight to your final destination, and if at any point during our journey you feel that our crew can make you more comfortable, please don't hesitate to call one of our wonderful flight attendants for assistance."

The intercom shut off and smooth jazz replaced the pilot's voice as the cabin crew prepared for takeoff. Overhead bins were opened and snapped shut all around Lucy, but she kept her eyes closed, breathing in the recycled air and trying not to flinch as someone bumped into her seat from behind. The person pulled at her headrest and jostled her as they got situated.

Think about Morocco, she told herself, inhaling and exhaling slowly. Lucy tried to imagine herself wandering through the outdoor markets, bargaining with vendors for pairs of colorful leather slippers, bright woven rugs and blankets, and gorgeously patterned dishes and pottery. She thought about the baskets of spices and pyramids of produce she'd find there, and pictured the azure blue of the buildings and the water. She couldn't wait to take in the rich culture and history of Marrakech, Casablanca, and Tangier.

As the images slipped through her mind, Lucy felt herself relaxing. Jason or no Jason, she'd still soak in the trip and do her best to meet the needs of her guests. His presence wouldn't throw her because she couldn't afford to let it.

The plane backed up from the gate and began to taxi while Lucy ran through the evening before one more time, then she put Dev away where he belonged and thought about Nick instead. As the plane picked up speed, she imagined the pictures she'd take in Morocco to send to Nick, and the souvenirs she'd buy to take home. It was going to be an amazing trip.

The next time Lucy opened her eyes, the pilot had signaled that the cabin crew was free to move around and deliver beverages. She lifted her head from her seat and looked out the window, feeling much calmer than she had before her flight to Venice; three trips in and she was already an old travel pro.

"Champagne?" a flight attendant asked, leaning toward Lucy with a tray of champagne in flutes.

"Yes, thank you," Lucy said, taking one and holding it in her hand as she turned her head to look at the clouds beneath her one more time. "Cheers," she whispered to herself, taking a sip and smiling contentedly.

For the moment, every man in her life—past and present—was on the ground, and she was up in the air, winging her way to a new continent, a new adventure, a new destination.

Lucy finished her champagne and then pressed the overhead button to request another.

Ready for the next book in the Holiday Adventure Club Series?

Join the Holiday Adventure Club as they tour Morocco on camels, camp under the stars, and find love and friendship in Africa. Buy it today from your favorite bookstore here!

About the Author

Stephanie Taylor is a high-school teacher who loves sushi, "The Golden Girls," Depeche Mode, orchids, and coffee. She is the author of the Christmas Key books, a romantic comedy series about a fictional island off the coast of Florida, as well as The Holiday Adventure Club series.

https://redbirdsandrabbits.com

Also by Stephanie Taylor

Stephanie also writes a long-running romantic comedy series set on a fictional key off the coast of Florida. Christmas Key is a magical place that's decorated for the holidays all year round, and you'll instantly fall in love with the island and its locals.

To see a complete list of the Christmas Key series along with all of Stephanie's other books, please visit:

Stephanie Taylor's Books

To hear about any new releases, sign up here and you'll be the first to know!

Made in the USA
Columbia, SC
05 March 2024

32682041R00089